Sleep was a cocoon
that protected her

"Time to go," he said huskily as her dazed eyes met his.

"Yes," she whispered, still drowning in his searching glance. "I suppose it is." She tried to speak lightly. Then he bent his head and his arms went around her.

She had wanted to protest, but as soon as she opened her mouth the flames springing up inside her consumed her. When Brent began kissing her passionately, she was lost beyond recall. She had had no time to accumulate enough experience to successfully counter his, and her initial defiance died with her last inclination to resist him.

If she had shouted, "I love you," at the top of her voice, she couldn't have told him anything her traitorous response wasn't already telling him loudly and clearly.

MARGARET PARGETER
is also the author of these

Harlequin Presents

and these

Harlequin Romances

Many of these books are available at your local bookseller.

For a free catalog listing all titles currently available,
send your name and address to:

HARLEQUIN READER SERVICE
1440 South Priest Drive, Tempe, AZ 85281
Canadian address: Stratford, Ontario N5A 6W2

MARGARET PARGETER

clouded rapture

Harlequin Books

TORONTO • NEW YORK • LOS ANGELES • LONDON
AMSTERDAM • PARIS • SYDNEY • HAMBURG
STOCKHOLM • ATHENS • TOKYO • MILAN

Harlequin Presents first edition April 1983
ISBN 0-373-10588-6

Original hardcover edition published in 1983
by Mills & Boon Limited

CHAPTER ONE

'It never rains but it pours!' Frank Martin exclaimed grimly. 'We no sooner get rid of the nephew than the great man himself appears. Talk about a summer shower!'

More like a thunderstorm, by the tone of Frank's voice! Startled, Sari Martin turned her head to gaze wide-eyed at her brother as he loomed suddenly in the stable doorway. 'Whatever are you on about? You don't mean Santo's uncle?'

'You're quite right to be suitably impressed, love,' Frank nodded dryly. 'I give you full marks for guessing, but it might have been more help if you'd been around with a length of red carpet. Brent Holding is in the house now and Anna's in a flat spin. You'd better come and see what you can do.'

'Me?' Sari's bewilderment turned swiftly to consternation. 'Oh no, thank you,' she laughed, suddenly refusing to take Frank's suggestion seriously, 'I'd rather keep out of the way, if you don't mind. I don't suppose he even knows about me, and I expect he's just passing through.'

'If that were all,' Frank replied tersely, 'I wouldn't be asking you to meet him. But he's here to stay, at least so he says, and he has a girl with him.'

'A girl?'

'Well, a woman,' Frank allowed in his ponderous fashion. 'I don't think she's all that young, but she's not so very old, either. He's demanding lunch and rooms. You name it and he wants it, pronto!'

'What a nice character he seems to be!' Sari's slender brows rose as she returned her saddle with a rueful sigh to the tackroom. 'He doesn't sound a bit like Santo.'

'He isn't!'

5

Sari frowned, her brother's heavy retort making her uneasy. 'How can you be so sure when he's never been here before?'

'He has been here before, but you've only been with me six months,' Frank explained with a kind of taut patience. 'He was left this place, but he's a busy man, especially, I believe, since his brother died.'

'He hired you through an agent and left you more or less alone for years. Had he any particular reason for his first visit?'

'To meet me, I suppose,' Frank grunted. 'It was long overdue, but he only stayed a few hours.'

'And what do you suppose are his reasons this time?' Sari drawled with mild sarcasm.

Frank shrugged. 'Maybe he just wants to relax for a day or two, and if Santo painted him a picture of rural tranquillity it might have put ideas in his head— who knows? Anyway,' he glanced at Sari meaningly, 'who am I to question my bread and butter, especially when it's so thickly spread with jam. You'd better come with me.'

Again she demurred, unable to explain her odd reluctance, even to herself.

Frank cast a knowledgeable eye over Sari's stubborn young face and sighed. 'It might be advisable, not just for my sake, or Anna's. I'd like you to make a good impression. He doesn't know my sister is one of his employees. It's something I forgot to mention—I don't know why.'

'You know why!' Sari bit her lip, feeling anxious for the first time. 'You were scared he wouldn't have me!'

'I do have the authority to employ my own staff,' Frank protested feebly.

'As long as the books show a good profit,' Sari muttered.

'If they haven't, this last year, it has nothing to do with you. No one could even suggest it.'

'But he might say you couldn't really afford me.

Remember I told you I would work for nothing but my keep?'

'What I give you is my business,' Frank said shortly, 'You certainly earn what you get and more.'

'He might not think so?'

'So now's your chance to convince him,' Frank smiled, his usual good humour returning; 'If the lady he has with him is as good in bed as she looks out of it, we might have nothing to worry about,' he added cynically.

Sari felt flags of colour edging under her fine skin. 'Do you have to make remarks like that, Frank?' she snapped.

'Sorry, love,' he grinned, amused by her obvious embarrassment, 'I forget how young you are.'

Suspiciously she stared at him. 'I suspect you were trying to give me some sort of hint. Just what kind of man is Brent Holding?'

'I'm not sure,' Frank replied, still grinning, 'but if you're half prepared it might at least save your blushes. If you catch him coming from milady's room through the night, just look the other way.'

'I'm not as innocent as all that!' she retorted dryly while trying to conceal a shiver of distaste.

Frank's ironic glance didn't give her the benefit of the doubt, but she managed to hide her resentment. She could see he was uneasy, despite his jesting. When a salesman from a commercial firm they dealt with swept into the stable yard and he groaned aloud, she said quickly,

'You go and see to him. I'll go straight to the house after I've put Sheba back in her field. No use leaving her to kick her heels in here when I might not be back.'

When Frank departed, still with an extremely harassed air, Sari led the horse slowly along the grassy lane to the pasture. Frank was a dear and she hated seeing him worried. He had a good job as manager of Carnford, a medium sized estate of some six hundred acres, but his last year he had had problems which unfortunately reflected in lower profits. This must be why Brent Holding was here, she decided scornfully. He was reputed to be extremely wealthy, but the more money some men made, the more they hated losing even a penny!

Frowning, she remembered Frank saying he wasn't like Santo, but of course he couldn't be. Santo was twenty, the same age as herself, and hadn't an ambitious bone in his body. When Santo had arrived, sent by his uncle to spend the few remaining weeks of his summer vacation, neither she nor Frank had known what to expect. Sari smiled, recalling how anxious they had been, but they needn't have worried. Santo—his mother had been Italian—was dreamy, unworldly, young for his age and very nice. Both he and Sari had enjoyed those few weeks immensely. Frank, struggling through a difficult harvest, had relied on her to keep Santo happy, and it had been a little like entertaining a child. They had ridden and driven about the countryside. Santo, seemingly incapable of making a decision, had left it to Sari to decide what they would do each day. They had talked and laughed and become warm friends, but nothing more. This was why he had startled her by weeping when he left and declaring he loved her. She had placated him tactfully while refusing to take him seriously, not even when he had sworn he would return and marry her.

This had happened over a week ago, and as she hadn't heard from him since she had relaxed with a private sigh of relief, putting the responsibility for his emotional outburst down to his volatile, half Italian nature. The arrival of his uncle was something of a shock. Sari bit her lip as she persuaded Sheba gently into her field and closed the gate. He could be here with a message from Santo, but common sense told her otherwise. From the odd bits of information Santo had dropped he didn't seem to be the kind of man who ran errands for other people, no matter how near or dear they might be. No, it had to be something Frank had done, something Mr Holding considered required his personal attention. Suddenly apprehensive, Sari ran swiftly back along the lane towards the house.

Indoors she was met by Anna with a long face. Immediately Sari entered the kitchen she began grumbling.

'If only Mr Holding had let us know he was coming!' she complained. 'Now there's two extra for lunch and no time to prepare anything. I'm a housekeeper, not a magician. I wish people would remember.'

'Oh, Anna!' Sari smiled. 'You know we often have to cope with half a dozen at a moment's notice. Heat some extra soup—the homemade tomato would be nice. There's plenty of steak and vegetables, and get Henry, if you can find him, to bring some fresh lettuce from the garden.'

'What about a sweet?' Anna was relying heavily on Sari now, preventing her from leaving. 'What do you think they would like?'

Sari ran distracted fingers through her mop of red-gold curls, praying for patience. 'Open two tins of peaches. I'll come back and whip some cream and decorate them up a little, after I've said hello to Mr Holding, but they might only want coffee.'

'Are you sure that will do?' Anna gazed at her dubiously. 'He mightn't mind something plain and simple, but she looks a proper madam!'

Recalling how Frank had referred to Brent Holding's girl-friend as milady, Sari asked shortly, 'Doesn't she have a name?'

Anna nodded, wrinkling her brow. 'Yes, but I've forgotten it. It's something outlandish I didn't quite catch. Miss de something or another. I'd be much obliged if you'd find out and tell me. I wouldn't want to be dismissed for not remembering.'

Sari sighed. 'Where are they now?'

'Your brother was talking to them in the drawing-room,' Anna informed her. 'I heard him saying you would be there directly.'

'I'd better go, then.' Sari glanced at her blue jeans doubtfully. 'Maybe I should change first?'

'He's already rung twice!'

Sari frowned. 'Santo was never impatient.'

'This man is different.'

So Frank had said, but how different? Sari wondered anxiously about this as she made her way through the rambling old house towards the drawing-room. Anna enjoyed sounding ominous. She might simply mean he was older? If he was Santo's uncle, he must be at least middle-aged?

Catching a glimpse of her untidy head in a mirror in the hall, she hoped the woman he had with him was beautiful enough to make him blind to another girl's lack of charm. But if he was disappointed, he had only himself to blame! Unexpected visitors couldn't expect to be met by someone in immaculate condition, and it wasn't as if she was the official hostess. She was merely his manager's sister, a girl he hadn't even known existed. Feeling more aggrieved by the minute, Sari thrust open the drawing-room door with more haste than grace, almost falling through it.

The man who was pacing up and down the large room bore every resemblance to a caged tiger and didn't appear particularly impressed by her somewhat clumsy entrance. He glanced over her swiftly, as though he was used to making a lightning inventory. It was only when he reached her face that his glance slowed and became more intent. What he found so interesting about her she had no idea, but he studied her face until she shivered convulsively and managed to utter a rather strangled, 'Good morning.'

'At last!' he exclaimed, as her husky voice broke the silence. 'You are Miss Martin, I presume?' Barely giving her time to nod, he continued curtly, 'I don't know where your brother's got to, but I don't appreciate being kept waiting.'

'I'm sorry,' for Frank's sake Sari forced herself to

apologise but met his cold, dark eyes with equally cool green ones. 'And you're Mr Holding I presume?'

His mouth tightened at what she could see he considered impertinence and, as her brief bravado faded, she silently reprimanded herself for being so foolish. Hadn't Frank enough worries without her adding to them by antagonising his boss?

But before she could mutter another apology, he said quietly, 'Yes, I'm Brent Holding, as I imagine your brother told you, and this,' he gestured abruptly, 'is Miss de Courcy.'

Miss de Courcy merely raised thin pencilled brows as Sari turned to gaze at her curiously. Ignoring Sari's polite smile, she went back to her bored contemplation of the fireplace.

Brent Holding continued looking at Sari and though his face was expressionless she knew he was angry. He was tall and towered over her and she could feel the tension in him. It began affecting Sari too, making her oddly breathless.

'What can I do for you?' she asked, anxiously trying to control herself.

'I'd like to see what accommodation there is,' he said coldly. 'I didn't get farther than the ground floor on my previous visit, and Miss de Courcy is tired.'

Poor Miss de Courcy! Sari thought dryly, her green glance going to the other girl's languishing figure. She didn't look as though she'd done a day's work in her life, though such superb elegance wouldn't be achieved without a lot of effort. Not a hair of her beautifully coiffured head was out of place and her make-up was so perfect Brent Holding must have to ask permission before he touched her.

Unaware that her fleeting contempt had shown on her face, Sari started guiltily when he spoke to her.

'I regret having to interrupt such pleasant thoughts, Miss Martin, but I don't want to stand here all day. No wonder the estate is doing so badly if this is the rate you get things done!'

Sari flushed, knowing she deserved his censure but resenting his cutting remark about the estate. While it confirmed her suspicions that it was falling profits which had brought him here, she was unhappy because of Frank.

Not trusting herself to reply, she stretched her lips in what she hoped passed for a repentant smile and led the way upstairs. Yet, as they went, her anger swiftly transferred from the arrogant man stalking behind her to Santo and Frank. Why had they allowed her to believe Brent Holding was elderly? He couldn't be more than in his thirties, and though not strictly handsome was striking, with his crisp black hair and dark, aloof eyes. Santo had said his uncle was single but no hermit—a fact born out by the presence of Miss de Courcy, but she wished Santo had been a little more explicit. She could feel Brent Holding's eyes boring in her back as she walked ahead of him and felt suddenly frightened.

At the top of the wide flight of stairs she turned, strangely confused, not quite knowing what to do. Was there some unwritten procedure regarding this kind of thing?

Conscious of her heightening colour, she looked straight at Brent Holding and drew a deep breath. 'The master suite is always ready, although you've never occupied it, I believe. I don't know where you want Miss de Courcy. Perhaps you'd like to see the rest of the rooms and decide for yourself?'

He returned her slightly challenging glance levelly. 'I'd like to see everything, Miss Martin, and we'll let Miss de Courcy decide.'

He betrayed not a flicker of discomposure, but his eyes glinted and Sari knew he was not unaware of what was passing through her mind. To hide her increasing embarrassment, she swung sharply around, marching stiffly along the corridor to the east end.

'When Frank first came he converted an attic on the top floor for himself, but I sleep here.'

Abruptly she opened the door of her own room, expecting Brent Holding would merely pop his head around it, but he startled her by strolling inside.

'Very nice,' he said, pausing in the middle of the floor to survey the walnut furnishings, which included a comfortable double bed.

To Sari, his tone seemed to imply it was too good for a mere employee, and, because it made her indignant, she was impatient to hear herself explaining. 'I had to sleep somewhere and Anna—Miss Morton said when Mr Mead, your uncle, had guests no one liked this end of the house as it gets no sunshine.'

Brent Holding shrugged his broad, immaculately clad shoulders without apparent interest. Picking up a photograph of Sari and Santo, he appeared to forget all about the room. It was a snap Santo had asked one of the farm boys to take of the two of them sitting on a bale of straw. Sari was laughing at something Santo had said and he had put his arm around her when Henry had asked them to sit closer together so he could get them both in. A few days later, when the film was developed, Santo had given her the photograph, and she had been startled to see they looked like a pair of lovers. She had accepted it reluctantly, rather than hurt his feelings, but had put it on top of the high chest of drawers in her room and forgot all about it.

Brent Holding gazed at it keenly, then laid it down again. He made no comment and she decided not to either. She felt uneasy, but realised in time that it might be unwise to jump to too many hasty conclusions. He might not be condemning her. He might even be gratified to discover his shy, retiring nephew was as capable as he was of getting close to a girl.

After a few moments, while Miss de Courcy waited with obvious boredom in the doorway, he motioned for Sari to carry on. She showed them five other rooms, then said that was all, apart from his suite.

'I like the pink one,' Miss de Courcy spoke at last. In a thin, fretful voice, she addressed Brent Holding. 'Really, darling, I'm exhausted! If you don't want me with you I think I'll have a shower and rest for a while.'

'Yes, of course.' Sari watched as he politely escorted his girl-friend back to her chosen quarters and left her. His attitude, though courteous, could hardly be described as lover-like, but Sari supposed he reserved his tenderness for moments when they were alone.

'Now,' he said, his long strides bringing him swiftly back to her, 'show me mine.' When Sari pointed uncertainly towards it, he took her arm, commanding more sharply, 'You'd better come with me.'

She had no other option but to do as he asked, especially as he almost dragged her into the suite and closed the door.

He didn't release her but turned to her with a charming, if taunting smile which renewed her former apprehension. While his brilliant glance raced over her again, she couldn't tell if he viewed her small, taut face with any pleasure. She read only mockery in his eyes as they lingered on her thick lashes and winged brows, her straight little nose and full, rather wilful mouth.

'I can't stay here!' she gasped, unable to explain, even to herself, her sudden, urgent desire to escape. 'I—I have work to do. Besides,' unthinkingly, 'Miss de Courcy mightn't like it.'

'Gloria never makes a nuisance of herself,' he replied smoothly. 'She knows the score, which is more, perhaps, than you do.'

He talked in sophisticated riddles, and she wasn't going to put herself out to follow him! She wasn't sure what kind of relationship he shared with Miss de Courcy, and Miss de Courcy was obviously worldly enough to know what she was doing, but Sari was determined she wouldn't be involved, any more than was absolutely necessary. She wanted nothing to do

with their sordid little affair! In a way she felt quite
sorry for Gloria de Courcy, for Sari didn't for a
moment believe Brent Holding was serious about
her. As his fingers tightened on her bare arm, she
cried angrily, 'I'm not so easily shocked, I'm just not
interested in what you do. Now please, Mr Holding,
will you let go of me?'

'When I'm good and ready,' he muttered, a threat in
his voice which caused her heart to lurch. 'Once you've
controlled that temper of yours and answered a few
questions, but not before.'

As Frank's boss—as hers, he was within his rights,
she supposed. Reluctantly Sari nodded her head, so the
red curls danced and the sunshine coming through the
window caught them, turning them to gold. 'All right,'
she mumbled sullenly.

'Well,' he smiled again, and it was still tauntingly,
'having got this far, how long have you been here?'

'At Carnford?'

Guessing she was playing for time did nothing to
soften the hard angles of his face. 'Yes,' he snapped.

'About—about six months,' she replied, suddenly as
instinctively wary as a young vixen, her red head up,
ready to flee.

'And before that?'

Defensively she lowered dark lashes to her cheeks for
fear he read more from her expression than she wanted
him to. 'I was in London,' she faltered.

She had been for over a week, living with Cilla—a
week she would never forget. She didn't want to tell
Brent Holding about this, or about the house in
Cornwall, where Frank and she had been brought up
by their aunt after their parents died. When Aunt Joan
had died after years of ill health, Sari had locked up the
cottage and gone to London, hoping to find work.

'London?' cynically Brent Holding interrupted her
painful thoughts. 'So why did you come here?'

Without putting it in words, he seemed to suggest

there must have been a less than desirable reason why a girl of her age should leave the excitement of the city to bury herself in the country.

Again she found herself curiously reluctant to explain anything to this man who obviously wanted to know everything! Hastily she improvised.

'Frank needed someone, a Girl Friday, if you like, and as I was out of work I thought it would be a change.' Better a little white lie than to confess she had been completely out of her depth in her cousin's ultra-modern flat and life. When Frank had arrived to rescue her she was unable to hide her tearful relief. Now she just wanted to forget all about it, and Frank's scathing remarks, as he had viewed the chaos wrought by the previous evening's party which Sari had spent locked in her bedroom, wouldn't bear repeating either. She hadn't argued when he had furiously packed her things, before packing her in his car and bringing her here, to Carnford.

'I see,' Brent Holding's curt voice jerked her back to the present. 'I don't suppose,' he drawled, 'it occurred to him to consult me?'

'If you mean about employing me,' she said, trying not to feel alarmed, 'Frank always hires his own staff.'

'I realise,' he nodded, 'but you're his sister.'

'What difference does that make?' she asked defiantly. 'He pays me for what I do, nothing more—or extra. I've never tried to take advantage of the situation, if that's what you're hinting at.'

'That's not what I'm hinting at,' he snapped, subduing her rising temper with a quelling glance. 'And for your future information, Miss Martin, I never hint! Regarding the staff here, your brother certainly has the authority to employ whom he likes, but I strongly object to arriving here and finding my house filled with his relations.'

'But there's only me.'

'It's a start,' with a sneer.

'Frank and I are orphans.'

'A lot of people are at your age,' he retorted unpleasantly.

Sari felt like hitting him. With an effort she kept her hands by her sides. Was there no way of denting such steel-like inflexibility?

'I'll move out. I'll find digs in the village,' she offered, thinking anxiously of Frank.

'As the nearest village appears to be miles away, what sort of a Girl Friday could you be living there?' While Sari sought desperately for an idea which might appease him, he asked slowly, his manner almost guarded, 'When will you be returning to London?'

'I'm not! That is,' she amended hurriedly, 'it depends.'

'Depends on what?'

Sari looked away from him in confusion. She wasn't sure what—it depended on herself. Unless it was how her remaining here might affect Frank's future. But if she said so, mightn't it give Brent Holding a sharper sword to wield over her head? If she kept quiet and waited a few days he might forget all about it— especially if, as Frank said, Miss de Courcy proved an attractive enough diversion?

'I'd rather not say,' she flushed.

His mouth tightened, as if he was coming to conclusions he didn't like. Sari waited, watching him, her heart beating unsteadily with apprehension. He was extremely attractive. His face was hard, his chin jutting, his mouth sensuous but disciplined. A man of strong passions, she suspected, both in temper and where his emotions were concerned, but always in control. It might be expecting too much to hope that any woman might be able to divert him.

She wasn't aware that she was staring until he spoke. 'Do you like what you see?' he asked, his voice suddenly softer but more calculating.

The flush which had began fading from Sari's face returned with a vengeance, this time consuming her whole body until she felt hot all over. Involuntarily she shrank from the slight smile on the mouth she had been studying so intently. Totally embarrassed, she did nothing to hide the antagonism in her eyes as she strove to deny any impression he might have gained that she found him in any way attractive.

'I see you don't,' he mocked, as she declined to answer.

'Mr Holding,' she sighed, exhausted from having constantly to remind herself of her somewhat precarious position, 'I scarcely know you!'

'That could easily be remedied,' he said, stepping nearer.

As he placed his hands on her shoulders, she felt so startled she couldn't move. He had well kept hands, but she could feel the steel in them as he took advantage of the seemingly hypnotic effect he was having on her to draw her closer. His eyes were hard too, as they met her widening ones, and she saw they were grey, whereas before she had thought they were black.

He must have felt how she was beginning to tremble and his glance softened, as if it was no part of his plan to frighten her. 'It must be very lonely here for a girl like you,' he observed, one of his hands leaving her shoulders to gently encircle her slender neck. 'Do you miss Santo?'

While she gasped at his unexpected query and tried to pull herself together, he deliberately tilted her chin and his mouth swiftly descended. As his lips swooped on hers and crushed them, a wave of incredible pleasure swept over Sari, almost swamping her. His fingers burned her sensitive skin and with a whimpering cry she found herself clinging to him helplessly. Shock shivered along her melting limbs as she responded blindly to his hard male strength. When his arms tightened until his body seemed to merge with her own, she was conscious of nothing else.

New experiences, her aunt used to say, should always be treated with caution, and this was a new experience for Sari. She had been kissed before, but never like this.

Until now she had considered kissing vastly overrated. As for going to bed with a man, she had vowed she never would, not unless she loved him and they were married. She had never suspected such sensations as she was experiencing now existed. As Brent Holding's mouth took possession of her lips and dealt with them slowly and sensuously, a finger of flame flickered deep within her before leaping to a consuming blaze.

It wasn't until he put her suddenly from him that Sari remembered her aunt's warning and came to her senses. She realised, if she hadn't been so vulnerable she might have struggled and escaped him sooner!

Shame stung her sharply as she exclaimed fiercely, 'You shouldn't have done that!'

His smile, as he stared at her angry face, was slightly whimsical. 'I often find the things I shouldn't do the most amusing.'

Sari gritted her small white teeth and winced when it hurt. Santo's uncle was no gentleman! He not only did despicable things, he said them as well! When he reached out, as if to pull her to him again, she slapped his arm away wildly.

'Did you make a habit of repulsing Santo, too?' he asked.

She didn't notice that this time the amusement in his voice didn't reach his eyes. 'Santo is—was different,' she retorted, not really thinking of Santo at all.

'He enjoyed being here,' his uncle shrugged lightly. 'When are you planning to see him again?'

The way he spoke gave no hint that he wouldn't approve. She had no plans to see Santo again, but it might pay to be diplomatic. Brent Holding seemed a man with his fair share of pride. If he suspected she was well on the way to despising both him and his nephew, he might have no compunction about getting rid of her.

'When Santo wants to see me,' she answered, hoping anxiously, as she recalled their last meeting, he never would.

Brent Holding appeared to take the nervous twist of her lips for a secret smile, and it angered him. 'You certainly don't believe in playing hard to get,' he snapped. 'Somehow I got the impression you were a girl who would take a lot of persuading. Or was that display of indignation a few minutes ago just for my benefit?'

Because he sounded so disparaging, Sari retorted tensely, 'Santo is very nice.'

'But still wet behind the ears so far as girls are concerned.'

Poor Santo, no wonder he had so little confidence when his uncle went round voicing such opinions! Oddly defensive, she muttered, 'He has a lot to offer.'

'There's no doubt about that!'

Suddenly Sari felt furious, and, as often happened when she lost her temper, she forgot all about being discreet. 'Mr Holding,' she blazed softly, 'you sent Santo to Carnford obviously to get rid of him, and because you didn't want him enjoying himself with girls in London. But wouldn't it have been wiser if you tried setting him a better example yourself?'

His eyes glittered frostily. 'Miss Martin,' he rapped back, 'when I require your advice I'll ask for it! And I doubt if you know what you're talking about. No one sent Santo here. I merely suggested it, although, believe me, I shouldn't have done even that if I'd known you would be around to help him wallow in self-pity.'

'I didn't help him do anything, except pass the time,' Sari faltered, decidedly confused. 'Someone had to entertain him and Frank was too busy, but we never talked much . . .'

Brent Holding taunted, 'He seems to have enjoyed himself all the same.'

'Yes,' she smiled, 'I'm sure he did.'

He looked down at her glowing head, his eyes darkening. Then his anger disappeared and he laughed. 'Perhaps it was as much my fault for putting temptation in his way.' His hand came up to tug at a tangle of red-gold curls. 'I should have checked first.'

Sari didn't follow. She found it difficult to think clearly with his fingers in her hair and his nearness making her tremble again. There was some kind of tension between them, and she was bewildered by the effect it was having on her. She felt she was being drawn by a magnet with ever lessening powers of resistence. Yet she was sure he liked her no more than she liked him.

Nervously she broke free of him and he let her go although, as if it pleased him to hurt her, he didn't release her hair until she winced.

'I apologise,' he said coolly, giving the impression he hadn't realised what he was doing.

She was certain he never made even a small move without being fully aware of what he was doing, but decided it might be wiser to retreat than attack. Soon, if she ignored him, he would get tired of baiting her. In fact he looked bored already.

'Going somewhere?' he muttered as she turned to leave him.

'Only to the kitchen, Mr Holding,' she replied, walking resolutely towards the door. 'Regardless of what you think, I have a job to do. I promised to help Anna with lunch, and if you want any you'll have to excuse me.'

'I could certainly do with something,' he remarked idly, managing to reach the door before her and hold it open. 'I had an early breakfast and a row in the office before I left, which is enough to give any man an appetite.'

'That sort of thing always ruins mine,' Sari said shakily, almost able to feel his breath on her face as he dismissed her with a slight inclination of his dark head as she walked past him.

CHAPTER TWO

SARI ran quickly downstairs, her feet barely touching the treads. Her heart was still beating too fast and she wanted a reason for it other than Brent Holding. If Anna noticed her cheeks were flushed she could now say it was because she had been hurrying.

Anna, however, was more interested in Brent Holding. 'Well, what do you make of him?' she asked eagerly.

Pans were bubbling on the stove. Sari ran an anxious eye over them as she tried to concentrate on two things at once. She liked cooking, but this morning her thoughts clung more tenaciously to the man she had just left.

'I'm not sure,' she glanced at Anna with guarded confusion in her emerald green eyes, 'but you were right when you said he isn't like Santo. Or did Frank say that? Anyway, there's a difference ...'

'There's a big one!' Anna sniffed, clearly favouring Santo's uncle.

Sari began carefully washing lettuce under the tap in the big stainless-steel sink. She liked the feeling of cold water running over her hands after the ordeal she had just been through. A puzzled frown creased her brow as she absently placed the clean leaves in a bowl. 'You worked for Mr Holding's uncle, Anna. Didn't Mr Holding ever visit Carnford while his uncle was alive?'

'Not that I can remember,' Anna replied, 'and I was with Mr Mead ten years. Of course the whole family was split by a terrible quarrel when Mr Holding would be a mere infant, and, as far as I can gather, no one ever tried to make it up. Mr Mead, being a widower, had everything left to his only child, but when Mr James was killed in one of those racing car accidents he changed his will in favour of Mr Holding.'

'Really?' Sari paused, surprised. 'When they didn't ever know each other?'

Anna shrugged her thin, drooping shoulders. 'Mr Mead said he didn't want the farm going out of the family and had heard enough about his nephew to be sure it would be properly looked after.'

'It does seem rather strange, though,' Sari mused.

'I suppose it might to you,' Anna agreed, 'but if Mr Mead didn't have anything to do with his relations he always seemed to know what they were up to. He was a difficult man in some ways, but a good one, all the same.'

'It's a wonder he didn't leave his money to charity,' Sari commented idly. 'A lot of people in his position do.'

'Oh, but he did,' Anna looked surprised. 'Didn't you know? Apart from five thousand pounds he left invested for me when I retire next year, the rest of his money was divided between his favourite charity and the church. Mr Holding just got the land.'

'I see.' Sari turned the tap off carefully. When she had mentioned Mr Mead's money she had really meant his estate, but Anna's remarks were enlightening. Brent Holding might have acquired the land for nothing, but he must have been obliged to put his own capital into it. This might explain why he was apparently so anxious it should be run as economically as possible. She wondered if Frank knew.

Lunch proved quite a success. If Miss de Courcy merely toyed with her food, ignoring anything solid, Brent Holding more than made up for her. He appeared to enjoy everything put before him and finished up with two cups of coffee. Sari wondered what Miss de Courcy did that she had to be so careful of her figure. Or was it simply that she imagined that to be attractive to a man like Brent Holding, a woman had to be thin to the point of emaciation?

They lunched in the dining-room. Frank had been told by the agent to use the whole house, if only to keep it aired, but usually they ate in the small breakfast room just off the kitchen. It was both more convenient and cosier. Sari had set places for three, but Brent Holding had insisted she joined them. She had agreed reluctantly, being strangely unwilling to see more of him than was absolutely necessary. Only Frank's pleading glance had stopped her from refusing. And something in the narrowed watchfulness of Brent Holding's eyes and the set of his mouth had warned Sari that he was not a man to be thwarted, in even such a small matter as this.

During the meal he disturbed her even more by glancing at her quite frequently, his gaze considering, as though he was trying to weigh her up. Sari found his close attention almost more than she could stand as it made her pulse race in a very peculiar way. It angered her too. She felt like asking him insolently if she had a smut on her nose, but somehow couldn't find the courage.

Although he didn't ignore Miss de Courcy completely, Sari didn't feel the rather distant smiles he bent on her proved he had any great affection for the girl and again she felt curious about their actual relationship. He talked mostly to Frank. Listening to him, Sari wasn't surprised to note how quickly Frank relaxed. While he might still be uneasy, regarding his boss's visit, most of his fears were obviously disappearing. Undoubtedly Brent Holding's charm had a lot to do with this, and, because she couldn't forget how she had reacted to it herself as he had kissed her, she found her own apprehension returning. For Frank's sake, she hoped Brent Holding's pleasantness wasn't being used to disguise something exactly the opposite.

After lunch, Miss de Courcy announced that she

would die of boredom if Brent didn't take her somewhere more lively for a while.

'You know I've always hated the country, darling!' she pouted, laying a possessive hand on his arm. 'We could go to Cheltenham.'

'You shouldn't have insisted on coming if you hate the country,' he retorted—Sari thought brutally, 'so stop whining.'

He did, though, agree to do as she asked and advised Frank that they wouldn't be returning to Carnford for dinner. 'Don't wait up for us,' he said. 'We may be late.'

They were late. Sari couldn't sleep, and it was well after midnight when she heard them come in. She had spent a quiet evening on her own, for Frank had gone out as well. He had had to attend a meeting, in connection with farming, and afterwards was taking his girl-friend out for a drink. Sari liked Lydia Newton, who worked for a local radio station. She was a pretty girl in her mid-twenties, full of fun and charming. Frank, who was over thirty, had never been as friendly with a girl before, and Sari wondered if he was thinking of getting married. This would be a wonderful house to settle down in and bring up a family. She wasn't sure what she would do if Frank got married? By then, perhaps, she might be ready to move on, though she couldn't think where to.

She blamed being slightly anxious about this for not sleeping. Frank looked in when he got home and said goodnight, but it seemed hours afterwards before Brent Holding's big car pulled up outside. Slipping quietly from her bed, Sari went to the window, but it was too dark and far away to see anything. She could only hear the distant murmur of voices. She waited until the same voices passed her door, then sped swiftly across the room and opened it.

She only opened it a mere slit, but was just in time to hear Brent Holding bidding Miss de Courcy a brief goodnight before they both disappeared into their respective rooms. Sari frowned as she absently closed her own door, thinking it rather strange behaviour for lovers. Then, as she remembered Frank's advice about snooping around in corridors, her cheeks flushed a guilty scarlet. She felt ashamed for allowing an overwhelming curiosity to persuade her into doing the very thing she had vowed not to.

The next morning she was down early, but it seemed not early enough. She felt quite stunned when Anna told her that Miss de Courcy had gone.

'Back to London,' said Anna, without apparent regret.

'B-both of them?' Sari stammered, fighting a heavy wave of despondency.

'No, only her,' Anna rattled the kettle as she filled it. 'He couldn't get a taxi, so he's taking her to the station himself. And,' her weighted words could have been nothing less than a hint, 'he'll be back any minute expecting his breakfast.'

Sari tried to think of bacon and eggs and failed. 'But why?' she asked blankly. 'I understood she was staying.'

'Don't ask me,' Anna shrugged. 'Here today, gone tomorrow, that's the way with high society. Not that she was ever that!' she added, with just enough emphasis to arouse Sari's curiosity.

'How do you know?' Sari realised she was rising to the bait beautifully but was unable to help herself. 'I thought you said you didn't know her?'

'I thought I didn't,' Anna agreed primly. 'It wasn't until I switched on the box last night that I remembered.'

'Is she an actress?' Anna was an inveterate watcher of television. In her younger days, strangely enough, she had worked in a famous London theatre and her interest in the stars had never waned. She had an amazing memory and never forgot a face, even if, as she grew older, it took her longer to place one.

'She plays small parts,' Anna smiled triumphantly.

'Has done for years, but she's never been famous. She told me this morning, when I took her up a cup of tea before she left, that the play she was in folded up the night before last. She didn't think it was all that bad, but hopes something better will turn up.'

While feeling sorry for Miss de Courcy, now she knew what had happened, Sari was nonetheless still bewildered. 'It seems strange that she should be rushing back to London like this—unless she has an urgent appointment?'

Anna said dryly, 'Between you and me, I think he's packed her off. Wasn't all that keen to go, if you ask me.'

Sari thought she had better not ask anything more about Gloria de Courcy. Imagining what Frank would have to say if he overheard them discussing her, she decided to drop the subject.

'We can't possibly know for sure why Miss de Courcy left, and perhaps we'd be wiser not to speculate. It might have been a different matter if it was something we'd done.'

While Anna maintained a doubtful silence, Sari began gathering together fruit juice and cereals to take to the dining-room. Secretly she wondered if Anna might not be right. She suspected Brent Holding was hard enough to get rid of a woman ruthlessly as soon as he lost interest, but she didn't think he would be so cruel as to force her to catch an early morning train. No, it was much more likely that Miss de Courcy had an appointment, and Mr Holding wasn't able to accompany her as he hadn't yet gone over the estate with Frank.

Everything was ready, the bacon and eggs piping hot when he returned from the station. He came into the dining-room alone while Frank went to wash his hands in the small cloakroom off the kitchen. Sari glanced at his tall figure, then concentrated on pouring orange juice after greeting him briefly. He was looking extremely fit, this morning, in a light sweater and darker pants. He was smiling and looked younger, he didn't have the appearance of a man who had just said goodbye to a girl he was particularly fond of.

Her heart skipped a beat as she glanced at him again and met the faint amusement in his grey eyes. She flushed as she suddenly knew he was aware of her speculation and what it was about.

He couldn't expect such unconventional behaviour not to arouse some speculation, but she wasn't sure that it was her place to mention Miss de Courcy's somewhat hasty departure. Sari didn't usually dither, but she had never felt quite so uncertain, and she had a horrid feeling it was now or never!

'I'm sorry I missed seeing Miss de Courcy before she left,' she said awkwardly at last, hoping this would suffice.

'Anna did all that was necessary,' he replied indifferently. 'What time do you normally rise?'

'Very early,' she answered stiffly, resenting the dryness of his voice.

'But not when you don't sleep?'

Sari flushed quickly. He couldn't possibly have heard her, she'd been as quiet as a mouse! He was merely guessing—or was he? 'I generally sleep very well,' she stammered, ready to sink through the floor with embarrassment.

'Oh,' he drawled blandly, 'I thought you didn't.'

Sari swallowed, afraid to say more for fear of ending up feeling even more humiliated than she did now. The slightly appraising smile on his dark face warned her she might never get the better of him in any argument, especially one in which he might easily hold the trump card. She was aware of his eyes going over her, taking in her thin shirt and jeans, the tender curves above her narrow waist. His glance lingered on them, then continued over her face and the soft, red-gold glory of her hair until she felt her whole body beginning to tremble. When Frank came in her relief was so great she nearly gasped.

'Hello, Sari,' he said casually, then frowned as though sensing the tension in the room. 'It's a lovely morning.'

'The sun's shining anyway,' she allowed.

He sighed, sitting down, reaching for the packet of cornflakes. 'I hope Sari's looking after you?' he said to Brent Holding.

'I'm surviving,' came the drawling reply, along with another mocking glance in Sari's direction.

Sari felt her blood boil when she thought of what he had already consumed, but her anger changed to a peculiar apprehension when Frank turned to him again and said, 'I'm afraid I have an appointment with my dentist this morning. I've just discovered it in my diary. I can cancel it, of course.'

'He had to cancel a previous one because of problems,' Sari exclaimed sharply, as Brent Holding's silence seemed to imply he was less than pleased.

'I'm quite capable of doing my own explaining, Sari,' Frank began.

Heedlessly she rushed on, 'You know how sore your tooth's been since you lost the filling.'

Frank spoke more firmly. 'I don't think Mr Holding would be interested in fillings—or problems which have now been solved.'

'Your brother's right, Sari,' Brent Holding intervened mildly, 'and I shouldn't dream of asking him to cancel another appointment,' he smiled lazily at Frank. 'I was going to suggest having a look round the estate but it can wait. I'm in no hurry. Unless,' he returned to Sari's frowning young face, 'you could take me?'

It was the last thing Sari wanted, to act as his guide. She met his raised brows nervously. 'I could,' she admitted, 'but I doubt if I could explain all the things you might want to know, and you might begin to feel I was wasting your time.'

'I was merely thinking of getting some fresh air,' he said, his mouth twisting sardonically at her obvious reluctance to accompany him. 'I'm quite capable of going on my own, but I'm not familiar with the estate boundaries.'

'I'm sure none of our neighbours would accuse you of trespassing, if you did get lost,' Sari smiled.

'Sari!' Frank almost groaned. 'Why don't you stop arguing and do as Mr Holding asks? Anna can manage quite well until you get back.'

'Would you rather ride or drive?' Sari enquired of Brent Holding, as they all went outside later.

'You'll see more on horseback,' Frank advised, as he went off to keep his appointment.

'It's a good morning for riding,' Brent Holding observed idly when Frank left them. 'Were those the horses I saw in the field as I arrived yesterday?'

'Yes ...' it suddenly struck Sari that he might consider them an unnecessary extravagance and she said hastily, 'They belonged to your uncle. They were here when Frank took over and he keeps them because they are handy. He rides a lot and they don't plough up the land in winter, the way heavy vehicles do.'

'They must be more time-consuming, though?'

'Not really,' she replied, eager to make him understand. 'You can take short cuts through woods with them, whereas you couldn't with a tractor, and you don't miss so much from the back of a horse.'

'They have a staunch advocate in you, anyway,' he laughed, the teasing amusement fading from his face as he looked down on her. With an effort Sari turned her head away as his eyes began penetrating hers and something flared in the depth of his, making her quiver. She felt confused and dismayed by the number of times he'd been able to do this when she'd known him less than twenty-four hours.

The estate didn't employ many full-time workers, and two of these were on holiday. On the lower ground tractors were busy ploughing the autumn stubble, but the higher fields were empty and quiet as they rode through them. They seemed to have the world all to themselves. The Cotswold hills were honey-coloured in the mellow September sunshine, basking in an atmosphere of contentment and peace. Frank loved it here—Sari suddenly swallowed a lump in her throat. If only Brent Holding didn't send him away.

Glancing at him anxiously, as he invaded her thoughts, she noticed how well he rode. She was no expert, but she knew he must have been familiar with horses all his life to be able to ride as well as he did. Spartan was only eight years old and it took Frank all his time to handle him, yet with Brent Holding he was being as good as gold. It was as if he realised the man on his back was boss and wouldn't put up with any nonsense. She recalled Santo rolling around in the saddle of the quiet old hack Frank had borrowed for him, and he hadn't improved. Still, she'd felt more at ease with Santo than she did with his uncle. Often she had been able to forget Santo was there, but she doubted if anyone could overlook Brent Holding, even for a few seconds.

On such a beautiful morning, however, it was difficult to continue feeling antagonistic. To Sari's surprise she soon found herself talking and laughing with him quite naturally. He watched her with a smile of appreciation in his eyes, but she wasn't sure if it was for herself or her horse or the way she rode.

'Who taught you to ride?' he asked as they cantered over a wide meadow.

'One of the men, after I came here,' she replied. 'Old Joe—there's nothing he doesn't know about horses. I expect you'll see him around.'

'So you didn't ride in London?'

'London? Oh, no.' She was puzzled until she remembered he believed she had lived there.

'You're remarkably good for a learner,' he said

softly, opening the gate at the far end of the field and allowing her to pass through before him, 'but do you really enjoy being a country girl?'

'I've always liked the country best,' she admitted, waiting idly while he followed her through the gate and closed it again.

'Santo doesn't.' He glanced at her coolly as they continued along a bridle path.

Why did he have to bring Santo into everything? It wasn't as if he appeared to be terribly fond of him?

'When he was here he seemed to like it well enough,' she frowned. 'If you weren't so strict with him, I think he might enjoy a lot of things better.'

'So he told you that, did he?'

His slightly incredulous tones didn't go unnoticed, but then people were often blind to their own faults. 'I suppose,' she allowed, 'it can't have been easy for you, having to bring Santo up—I mean since his parents died. You must have been very young yourself.'

'It was only ten years ago. I was twenty-five.'

And already capable of moving mountains—businesswise! Sari swallowed, moving on to what she considered safer ground. 'Parents have natural instincts . . .'

His expressive brows shot up as he slanted a mocking glance at her uncertain face. 'Are you trying to imply that I simply blundered on? I have natural instincts too, you know. If some are not yet fully developed, I can assure you they're all there.'

Sari's cheeks coloured slightly as something in his voice stirred her blood and made her disturbingly aware of parts of herself she never remembered existed. 'It might have been easier for Santo if you'd been married,' she said impulsively. 'A wife might have helped.'

'Sari,' the taunting gleam in his grey eyes deepened, 'not even for Santo will I sacrifice my freedom. Not when I like it so much. If he craves for a woman in his

life he must marry one himself—as he will do when the
time comes.'

'At least, in this, you must allow him to please
himself,' she pleaded, unaware of the hint of despair in
her voice.

'I think not,' he replied curtly.

Flushing with indignation, on Santo's behalf, Sari
didn't bother to hide her contempt. Then realising
Brent Holding was eyeing her with increasing coldness,
she forced herself to change the subject. If she had set
out to please him she was obviously going about it the
wrong way.

'When will you be returning to London, Mr
Holding?' she asked politely.

'The name's Brent,' he said, without altering his tone
or answering her query.

His apparent reluctance to discuss his immediate
plans brought a return of her former apprehension, and
although she tried not to let it show, she refused to be
sidetracked. Producing a rather strained smile, she
pointed out, 'There won't be enough to keep you
occupied at Carnford for more than a day or two.'

'I don't want to be occupied,' he returned her smile
lazily. 'I intend doing as little as possible, for the next
week or two.'

Sari's eyes widened with alarm. 'But not at Carnford,
surely?'

His eyes held hers for a long moment, as if he might
be willing to drown in such cool, dazzling greenness.
'Why not?'

'You'd be—bored.'

Brent ignored this. They were riding side by side and
he edged his horse expertly a little nearer, so he could rest
his hand just behind her saddle. 'I'd like to stay here,' he
said quietly, as she trembled, 'If I won't be in the way?'

He spoke so humbly Sari blinked with surprise, even
as she tried to control the strange feelings he aroused by
his unexpected action. She could have sworn he had

disliked her on sight. She was sure she had seen dislike in his eyes, even when he had been smiling at her. Now he was being quite friendly, he'd even gone so far as to suggest she called him Brent. Was it surprising, she wondered abjectly, that she wasn't sure what to think?

Then, suddenly, as she stared down at Sheba's glossy brown coat, she decided she was too full of doubts. She didn't know much about olive branches, but if Brent was holding one out, she might be a fool not to grasp it quickly. It certainly shouldn't do Frank any harm if they were friends, it might even help him a lot.

Her smile was a little mischievous but warm, as she turned to him again. 'I could hardly tell my boss he wasn't welcome, but it would be nice if you could stay—Brent . . .'

'Hmm,' his eyes held wry amusement. 'Well, it's a start. It took you long enough to make your mind up. Are you always so cautious, Sari?'

Carelessly she shook back a straying red-gold curl and the movement of her head, assisted by the wind, set the whole lot dancing. 'I'm not cautious, at all, that's my trouble.'

'I mean with men.'

'Oh,' her thick lashes swept her cheeks, making her look very young and charming, 'I haven't known a great many.'

Fleeting anger seemed to return, but when, sensing it, she glanced up in alarm, she only caught the end of it. Wryly Brent muttered, 'There's no such thing as an honest woman, but you're little more than a child.'

Whatever that was supposed to mean? Sari bit her lip in bewilderment. She couldn't keep up with his lightning changes of mood!

Shrugging off his last remark, she said, 'I suggested you might be bored because I didn't think you'd be all that interested in farming. I know you own Carnford and need to satisfy yourself it's being properly run, but it didn't occur to me that you'd want to stay long.'

'It might surprise you to learn,' he smiled, 'that my father had a farm for about twelve years. It was only a hobby, he had a manager and men, the same as I have here, and he sold it when I was in my teens. During those years, though, I managed to learn quite a lot, enough anyway to keep me interested.'

'But you don't live in the country now.'

Again a slight jeer. 'Didn't Santo tell you? I have a house in West Sussex with a few acres of land. I don't farm, I decided long ago my real talents lay in other directions. I was in partnership with my brother when he died.'

'It will be easier for you when Santo steps into his father's shoes.'

'That won't be for a while yet.'

Sari regretted having mentioned it. Not many minutes ago she had been wondering why he kept bringing Santo into the conversation, yet here she was doing the same thing herself. And when she mentioned Santo he seemed even angrier than when he spoke of him, himself. Inwardly, she was still convinced that the strain of bringing up a young boy must have been a heavy one. Perhaps that was why, despite what he also said about his freedom, he had never married. She had been quick to point out the advantages of a wife, but many women might object to having their husband's nephew as a more or less permanent fixture in their lives.

As they emerged from the woods to open country again, Sari felt Brent's hand leave the back of her saddle as he forged ahead. Swiftly she urged Sheba after him and was relieved when he allowed her to catch up. After this she concentrated on less personal matters, showing him as much of the estate as she could before lunch. She explained the boundaries and most of the fields, in relation to the house, until she was sure, if he was out on his own, he wouldn't get lost.

'You've only been here six months, yet you know the

layout remarkably well,' Brent Holding mused, as they
rode back to Carnford. 'Did you visit your brother
often before coming to live here permanently?'

'No,' she confessed reluctantly, 'Frank always came
to us. When he could get away,' she added hastily but
quite truthfully, 'because he's always so busy. When I
came to work for him, he said it would be useful to
know my way around. Sometimes when there's a
message to be sent to one of the men and he hasn't time
to go himself, he sends me.'

'I see.'

He sounded thoughtful but not disapproving. Sari
felt a little happier as they trotted on. Occasionally he
still shot her a sharp glance, but he didn't seem so ready
to snap at her. She began to relax and even enjoy his
company. He was stimulating, she discovered, in a way
Santo had never been, and she found herself stealing
frequent glances at him when she thought he wasn't
looking.

The sun was high overhead and hot by the time they
reached the stables. 'We seem to be having an Indian
summer,' Sari laughed. 'If you do intend staying it
looks as though you're going to be lucky with the
weather.'

Brent turned to look up at her, as she sat on her
horse, gazing around, her lovely face glowing with
contentment and good health. To her surprise, he held
up his arms, obviously to help her down. She had no
other option but to let go of Sheba's reins and slide into
them.

She had expected to be slightly embarrassed, but was
unprepared for the sudden rush of feeling that hit her
and raised startled, slightly bemused eyes as his arms
tightened briefly. The hand gripping her waist hurt, but
she tried not to flinch as she smiled at him and he
lowered his head.

She was sure he would have kissed her if Frank's car
hadn't, at that moment, swept into the yard behind

them? When he let her go, it was slowly and he was breathing as deeply as she was. It seemed to be some sort of reaction they triggered off in each other. Sari wasn't quite sure what it was, but it wasn't anything she had experienced before. Whatever it was it made her feel both nervous and excited—and strangely curious. Then, without a quiver of embarrassment, Brent smiled at her and, as old Joe came up to take his horse, he walked away from her to speak to Frank.

During the next few days Sari tried to keep out of Brent Holding's way as much as she could, but it proved impossible to avoid him altogether. It was for her own sake that she tried so deliberately to avoid him as she became increasingly aware of him and realised the folly of becoming more deeply involved. To begin with this wasn't too difficult. At mealtimes Brent talked mostly with Frank and spent most of his time with him, either in the office or touring the estate. Frank told Sari he had a brain like a computer and was going over everything with a small tooth-comb. When Sari was indignant, he actually grinned and said he was learning a lot and was enjoying the experience. It only surprised him that Brent Holding was sparing the time to help him personally. Most men, he said, would simply have delegated the matter to their agent, or told Frank to go.

'It's not as bad as all that, surely?' Sari's face paled. 'You haven't been doing something you shouldn't, Frank?'

'No!' His smile faded, but there was no expression of guilt, which she found reassuring. 'It's more a case of mounting costs and not knowing where to cut down. I haven't been paying enough attention to this side of things, but it's amazing what can be sorted out.'

He wouldn't say much more, but Sari was still worrying about it a few days later, as they all sat around the fire after dinner. She wasn't able to find a suitable excuse for not joining them every evening, as she had really nowhere else to go. She hoped

desperately that there was nothing much wrong with
Frank's management of the estate. He had been seeing
rather a lot of Lydia, perhaps this might explain his
neglect of the books, but he usually worked hard; he
hadn't even taken his annual holiday yet. But she
doubted if any of this would carry much weight if Brent
discovered a serious deficit anywhere.

'Do you usually go out much in the evenings?'
Brent's voice broke through her anxious thoughts,
making her start as he put the question to Frank.

When Frank didn't reply but looked at Sari, she
wondered uncomfortably if he had told Brent about
Lydia.

'I don't,' she replied quickly, as Frank remained
silent and his face coloured slightly. 'Frank does
though, occasionally,' she didn't say where.

'Why don't you go too?' Brent asked, his eyes flicking
over Sari's graceful figure deep in one of the old velvet-
covered armchairs. She was wearing a soft green dress
which made her eyes look even greener than ever and
her skin like alabaster. Her hair, rioting as usual in a
wealth of glowing curls, seemed to outrival the fire for
colour. Something stirred in his dark glance and then
was gone as she met his enquiring gaze warily.

'I—I haven't met many people since I came here—
there hasn't been time.'

'Why don't you take your sister out and introduce
her to some?'

He spoke so bluntly, Frank couldn't go on evading
an answer. 'I've offered,' he exclaimed in somewhat
righteous tones, 'but she prefers staying at home.' He
didn't mention that this was because Sari had no wish
to be an unwanted third, when he went out with Lydia.
He added, and she wished somehow he hadn't, 'She did
go out a lot with Santo.'

Brent's mouth tightened as he viewed her pink
cheeks. 'So you aren't anti-social altogether!'

Sari was about to tell him—let Frank be as angry as

he liked, she had been out in the evenings with Santo once, when the telephone rang from the hall.

'I'll take it,' said Brent, before either Sari or Frank could move. 'It must be the call I'm expecting.'

He was back in moments, however, saying it was a Miss Newton for Frank.

Frank hurried out, his face again a dull red, and Brent watched the door closing thoughtfully. 'Miss Newton?' he repeated, his brows raised in a query Sari was unable to avoid.

'A girl-friend.' She tried to speak casually, hoping, if he had more questions, he would wait and ask Frank.

But he wasn't a man willing to wait for anything, as she might have known. 'A girl-friend,' he mused, fetching his cup to Sari for more coffee. 'One of them— or the one?'

'I'm not sure.' Sari, having wondered herself, forgot about being discreet. 'I've never known him bother much with girls before, but he seems very fond of Lydia.'

'Is she a local girl?'

More cautiously, she replied briefly, 'Not really. She lives in Worcester and is very nice.'

Brent sat down again, lifting the cup Sari had refilled to his lips, glancing at her speculatively over the rim. 'What will you do if your brother gets married?' he asked tauntingly. 'You might only be in the way if you stayed on here.'

Because she had worried about this rather a lot lately, when Brent mentioned it, he touched a very raw spot. She wasn't trained for anything special and there was only London. Blindly fighting down an irrational panic, she muttered the first thing to enter her head, without quite realising what she was saying. 'Santo asked me to marry him and I refused, but I could always change my mind.'

CHAPTER THREE

SARI didn't look at Brent as he jerked to his feet and strode abruptly to the window. He muttered something under his breath, she wasn't sure what, but the crash of his coffee cup on the small table by the curtained alcove didn't sound too reassuring.

She felt slightly ashamed of herself, but thought it rather foolish of him to take her remark seriously. In a way, if she had angered him he had only himself to blame. He hadn't spared her feelings when he had taunted her about being a nuisance to Lydia and Frank. He might have known she would retaliate in the only way she could, but they both knew Santo was too young to be married. Some boys were mature enough for marriage at twenty but Santo wasn't one of them.

If she regretted anything it was telling him of Santo's proposal. She hadn't intended telling anyone, not even Frank, for although she hadn't taken Santo's offer of marriage seriously, she had no wish to have other people treating it with the amusement they might callously think it deserved.

She was anxiously trying to find the right words to explain this to Brent when Frank returned, and it was too late. Then she decided it didn't matter. Brent might not believe her if she did try and explain. It might be better to leave it to time to prove she had merely been joking.

Almost as soon as Frank entered the room the telephone rang again, and this time it was for Brent. While he was gone, Sari excused herself and went to bed. There didn't seem much point in holding a further discussion with Frank regarding the real purpose of

Brent's visit; they had already speculated too much. Perhaps the next few days would provide answers to the questions they were both reluctant to ask.

Physically Sari must have been tired, for in spite of restless thoughts, she fell asleep almost immediately. She wasn't sure what had awakened her, hours later, until she heard a faint noise. With a protesting groan she switched on the light and found Cindy, the farm cat, wandering back and forth across the carpet. She must have crept in earlier and been hiding somewhere. It was a favourite trick of hers, but now she was obviously ready for some nocturnal meandering. There was a hole in the bottom of the scullery door, which she used to escape from the house, but first she had to get out of Sari's room.

'Oh, you silly creature!' Sari exclaimed, gathering Cindy in her arms as she half rolled out of bed to give her a hug before popping her outside. 'You're a terrible nuisance,' she whispered, 'but I love you.'

She smiled, cuddling Cindy closely to her, gently tickling the soft, silky fur, and Cindy responded by purring complacently and rubbing her head against Sari's chin as she quickly opened the door.

Sari didn't know who received the greater surprise, she, or the man standing a few yards away along the corridor. But there was no doubt as to who was the first to recover.

Instead of going into his own room, Brent swung swiftly towards her. 'What the . . . ?' he began, then, 'Oh, good heavens, it's a cat!' As Cindy fled, after Sari had hastily dropped her, he threw back his dark head and laughed.

'It's only Cindy,' she stammered in startled confusion. 'I should have warned you she often hides in a bedroom.'

'Yours?' he asked, still smiling.

'Anybody's,' she sighed.

'I meant, is it your cat?'

'Oh, I see. No, she belongs to the farm——' Sari's voice trailed off as she suddenly became conscious of the laughter dying from his face as he began studying her intently and she remembered she was wearing only a thin nightgown. It was buttoned down the front, but unfortunately half the buttons had become undone when she had fallen out of bed to grab Cindy. It left her full, creamy breasts practically uncovered and she flinched as his eyes seemed to burn her bare flesh.

'Oh!' she flushed with shame, trying frantically to pull the gaping fronts of her nightdress together and retreat at the same time.

Brent allowed her to step backwards into her room, but no sooner was she inside than he followed. His movements were quick and quiet, not stumbling, like hers, and, as she retreated even farther, he closed the door and reached for her. She was aware, belatedly, that she would have been wiser to have stayed in the corridor.

'You can't come in here!' she whispered hoarsely.

'I'm already in,' mockingly he reminded her of the fact. 'Surely I can have the same privileges as a cat?'

'Oh, please,' her voice was husky, 'you know that's ridiculous!' Agitatedly she raised her hands to push him away and, in doing so, inadvertently released her nightdress. 'Oh,' she cried, almost choking with fright and temper, 'now look what you've done!'

'Leave it,' he commanded, his voice as husky as hers as she numbly began doing up buttons. 'I want to see you.'

'No!' she moaned, as he stared down at her and something in his glance sent sensation rocketing through her. Helplessly her voice died in a throat which went almost too tight to let her breathe. Her whole body trembled and she couldn't move.

'You're beautiful,' he groaned, his eyes devouring her soft, rounded curves and, as if unable to resist any longer, his mouth lowered to trace the delicate blue veins which led to pale pink tips.

When he lifted his head Sari was having even more trouble with her breathing, and when his mouth came down on hers, to her dismay she found her lips parting under his like the petals of a rose opening to the heat of the sun. He didn't hurt her, he was amazingly gentle, and every fibre of her body responded. The touch of his lips became nectar. She thought she was floating, yet her limbs felt suddenly heavy and she was sure she was going to fall.

Brent paused, his face dark and shadowy above her as he gazed at her, a slumbering fire in his eyes. 'You're lovely,' he repeated thicky, running a hand lightly over her delicate features, his fingertips touching her cheeks and closed eyes before tangling in her glorious hair.

Sari tried but could offer no resistance. She might have been bound hand and foot, so unable was she to even stir. She heard him catch his breath and felt his mouth against her neck, hard and searching in the hollow where her pulse beat madly.

His sudden switch from gentleness to passion released Sari's strange paralysis. Her arms crept around his neck, her fingers burying themselves in his thick black hair. When his mouth returned to take hers, this time his kisses were deeper, more demanding. Her senses swam as he pushed the opening of her nightdress wider and his hands slid underneath it. He softly caressed the smoothness of her back, the deep indentations of her spine and waist. Then his arms tightened and he pressed her against him so fiercely she almost cried with pain.

'Sari,' he gasped against her lips, 'don't you know how much you tempt me?'

His hoarse query broke the trance of her senses. Was she tempting him? It seemed like an accusation, and though she tried to ignore it she couldn't. Horror dawned in her eyes as she opened them and pulled away from him.

'I didn't do it deliberately,' she whispered.

His breath rasped. 'You encouraged me to come into your bedroom.'

'But I didn't!' her green eyes widened with angry resentment. 'I told you not to come in here!'

'Of course you did,' he snapped impatiently. 'It's all part of the game, isn't it? The initial protests, designed to make a man all the keener. I've never heard of a cat being brought into the act before, but I might have known you'd be more than a little ingenious.'

How could he say such things? What could she say to convince him how wrong he was? He stood staring at her, big, dark and powerful, sounding relentless. And he seemed to have his mind made up about women. Sari doubted if anything she could say might change it.

'I—I don't entertain men in my room,' she muttered helplessly.

There was disbelieving scorn in his eyes as he asked harshly, 'Did Santo never come here?'

She flushed. 'He only came in once—and then just for a few minutes.' She had been making her bed after breakfast, when the post arrived and he had sought her out, to give her the photograph.

She looked away from Brent briefly, suddenly afraid of the fury in his eyes, but when her glance was again drawn back to his face she found surprisingly that it had softened. He was a strange man, she thought with a quiver, wondering if she would ever understand him.

Swiftly he reached for her again, capturing her trembling body before she could move. 'I don't know how you feel about Santo,' he said sardonically, 'but you certainly responded to me. A woman might pretend, but there are some things she can't hide. You wanted to be in my arms as much as you were almost begging me to kiss you.'

'You're imagining things!' she panted, struggling furiously to be free. Yet despite her protests, she suspected he was very near the truth, no matter how much she tried to deny it. Even so, she had no wish to provide farther proof of the traitorous weakness of her own feelings.

Brent smiled lazily. 'This is no place to argue.'

His voice seemed to hold a sensuous threat and she struggled harder. 'Will you let me go!'

'If you kiss me goodnight.'

She almost gasped with surprise. Did he really mean it? They were alone at this end of the house and even if she screamed no one would hear her. Her heart still pounded, but she decided to take him at his word and raised her face obediently.

His smile disappeared as he bent again to kiss her lips, his mouth controlled, if a little tightly, Again, Sari was hit by a wave of searing emotion, and, to her shame, was beginning to cling when he put her firmly from him.

'Goodnight, Sari,' he muttered, thrusting her roughly aside and leaving the room without looking back.

The next morning he didn't come down until after Frank had gone out, and Sari wondered if he'd stayed in his room deliberately.

'Don't rush off, Sari,' he said, as she set a fresh pot of coffee in front of him, along with his bacon and eggs. 'I want to talk to you.'

Her cheeks went scarlet as she hesitated. Surely he didn't intend discussing last night?

From the glint in his eye he might have guessed what was passing through her mind. Cruelly he let her stew for a few moments in hot embarrassment while he poured himself a cup of coffee. Then he asked politely if she wasn't going to join him.

'I've had mine,' she said, hastily declining.

'Another cup won't harm you,' he glanced at her mockingly, as though well aware she felt in need of something.

'Thank you,' she mumbled, sitting down, thinking she might as well suffer in comfort.

She was so sure it was her shortcomings he was about

to mention that she almost fell off her seat with surprise when he remarked calmly, 'Your brother would like to get married.'

Sari stared at him. 'Frank?'

Curtly, Brent said, 'You only have the one that I know of.'

'Yes.' Sari bit her lip, disregarding his faint impatience. 'I'm sorry. When did he tell you?'

'After you went to bed.'

She sat fiddling with her cup, not realising how pale she had gone. She felt happy for Frank, but, at the same time, rather hurt that he had told Brent first. Of course, she reasoned, he would have to make sure his future was secure before he asked Lydia to marry him, and it made sense that he couldn't tell his sister or anyone else until Lydia had agreed.

Uncertainly she glanced at Brent, seeking confirmation. 'He hasn't asked Lydia yet?'

Brent buttered a slice of toast with maddening precision. 'Not yet,' he met Sari's anxious eyes enigmatically. 'He's going to wait until I reach a firm decision over Carnford.'

She thought she knew what he meant. Indignantly she jumped to her feet. 'You aren't being fair! I know profits are down, but it's just been a bad year. You can't sack a man because of that!'

'Sit down, Sari!' It was an order, given so sharply that she obeyed immediately, although she continued looking at him indignantly. Did he have to sit there, looking like a superior god? He was so assured, he forgot other men weren't always as decisive. But if Frank was inclined to dither, he was honest and his heart was in the right place.

'You might,' she exclaimed unsteadily, 'try a dozen men who would do no better than Frank. In fact, with some you might fare a lot worse. I'm sure he never tries to cheat you.'

'Have I ever said he did?'

Flushing again, she hoped she wasn't making matters worse. 'No,' she admitted reluctantly.

He seemed about to say something, but changed his mind. 'I have to decide, Sari,' he went on after a brief hesitation, 'whether Carnford is worth keeping or not.'

'But your uncle left it to you!' she interrupted. sharply.

'That was purely incidental,' he replied shortly, 'and I refuse to go over past history which had nothing to do with me. My uncle loved Carnford, but I doubt if he expected me to be as sentimental. I kept it as an investment, but I have no intention of retaining it if it doesn't pay. I have enough profitable interests elsewhere.'

'But what about Frank?' she choked.

'Sari,' he said bluntly, 'I don't want you weeping yet. Nothing's going to happen for the next few days.'

She made one last plea. 'You won't get rid of Carnford and Frank just because of last year?'

He gazed at her thoughtfully and sighed. 'I wasn't going to mention this, Sari, but I've had rather disquieting reports of last year. That profits fell off abysmally couldn't wholly be blamed on bad luck and bad weather. Frank has been away from the estate a lot, and not always on business.'

This was true. Sari's thick lashes fell unhappily. Several times while she had been here, the agent had called and Frank had not been available.

'Lydia works odd hours,' she confessed reluctantly.

'Exactly,' Brent nodded, as if he had already guessed. 'Unfortunately I have to decide if the situation is likely to improve once they're married. If Miss Newton keeps her job and continues working odd hours, it could mean Frank's life being permanently disrupted.'

'I think she would stop working after a few years and have a family,' Sari suggested eagerly.

'Am I supposed to find that comforting?' Brent asked derisively.

Sari stared at him angrily, feeling driven. 'Oh, why don't you just tell Frank to go,' she cried, 'and get someone else!'

'Because I don't want anyone else!' he snapped, 'Either your brother stays or I sell the place, it's as simple as that. Could he afford to buy it?'

'No,' she shook her head bitterly, 'but if I had the money I would buy it for him.'

'Would you?' he said indifferently, but she didn't see his eyes narrow suspiciously.

That evening Frank was going out, and later in the day Brent asked Sari if she would have dinner with him. If she agreed he would book a table.

Sari didn't feel like going anywhere with him, not after their conversation that morning, but she knew she must do everything she could to help Frank keep his job. She was wise enough to know that, even in this day and age, a decision could be swayed as much by a smile as logic. Not that Brent was likely to be influenced by such a thing as a woman's smile, she thought wryly, but she could always comfort herself that she had tried. And Carnford meant security for her too. Here she was safe, cocooned from the turbulence of the outside world. After sampling life in London, she had no wish to leave it, and if she tried to please Brent Holding he might relent and give Frank another chance.

With vague hopes spinning hazily in her mind, Sari forced herself to reply brightly that she would love to have dinner with him, and while his eyes gleamed with a faint scepticism, she was surprised to find she was speaking the truth. A glow of excitement spread through her and she knew she wasn't thinking wholly of Frank.

They drove to Cheltenham, some twenty miles away. The October evenings were drawing in, but the weather was still fine, making driving easy. Brent wore a dark blue lounge suit and in it he looked disruptively masculine. It was the first time Sari had seen him other than casually dressed since he came, and it made her uneasy that her heart beat faster every time she looked at him. His dark, striking looks made her realise he must be extremely popular with many women far more glamorous than herself, and she wondered why he was taking her out. While he might tolerate her, she didn't think he enjoyed her company all that much. They seemed on edge with each other most of the time, and although he appeared to derive some pleasure from teasing her, she wasn't convinced he enjoyed it enough to devote an entire evening to it.

Unless he was after entertainment of another kind and thought a good dinner, with soft lights and possibly music, might soften her up. In the darkness of the car, Sari flushed. He had kissed her twice, but both times it had probably only been because of provocation, and, as she was a woman, he had been unable to retaliate in any other way. In his bedroom, on the first occasion, he had been angry and could scarcely have hit her, and in her bedroom, last night, if she had provoked him differently, by appearing half naked, any man might have reacted as he had done, especially a highly sexed one. But she didn't want Brent to believe she was there for his amusement, for casual kisses any time of the day. When he was feeling bored, or slightly amorous, she must make it clear she wasn't here for the sole purpose of relieving such feelings, especially when any woman might do!

It was after eight when they reached Cheltenham. It was a lovely old town, one of the foremost spas in England and a famous centre for music, art and sport. Sari had only been here once before, but she recognised the name of the hotel where Brent had booked their dinner. Frank had once told her it was very good but expensive. Occasionally he and Lydia ate there, but more often they just called in for a drink after a show.

It happened they were there that evening, and Sari wished she had thought to warn Frank that this was

just the kind of place that Brent was likely to patronise.
They dined late and were just on their way to the
lounge for coffee when Lydia and Frank came in.

When Sari first heard Brent speaking to someone she
didn't immediately turn her head. Already she had been
rather startled by the number of people he had nodded
to, and was being forced to cancel the suspicions she
had had that he had only taken her out because he
knew no one else. This was an area where many wealthy
people lived, as well as a lot of the racing fraternity. She
might have known he would have friends here. She
wondered why he hadn't chosen to dine with one of the
rather gorgeous females who glanced at him with quite
undisguised longing in their eyes.

So she was surprised and rather embarrassed when he
laid a detaining hand on her arm and asked mockingly
if she didn't want to speak to her brother.

Frank grinned at her startled expression. 'Sari is
often in a daydream,' he observed with brotherly
candour. Then he was introducing Lydia to Brent, and
briefly Brent's attention left her again.

Lydia was smart, with plenty to say for herself, but
underneath her surface gaiety was a warmth and charm
which Brent soon seemed to discover and appreciate.
Lydia's dress, Sari decided ruefully, put hers in the
shade. She went out so rarely, and unfortunately,
because Brent's invitation had come so late, she had
had no time to shop for something smarter than the
creamy pale chiffon she wore. She had only worn it
once before, and while hanging in her wardrobe might
have preserved it, it didn't seem to have improved it. If
Brent's glance had rarely left her during the meal they
had shared, she suspected it was her red-gold hair and
bare shoulders which had attracted his attention, rather
than the somewhat limp creation she was wearing.

The only jewellery she possessed was a necklace
which had belonged to her mother. Her aunt had said it
was quite valuable but needed to be reset. As Sari had

never been able to afford to have this done, she wore it as it was. And, on the rare occasions when she did wear it, she had no idea how effective the green stones looked against the smooth white skin of her neck.

Brent, after the preliminaries were over, asked Frank if he and Lydia would care to join them. Sari felt glad when they accepted. At least, she thought, Brent had met Lydia, without it seeming contrived, and she didn't see how he couldn't approve of her. If he had been anxious regarding the suitability of Frank's future wife, then this meeting must surely set his mind at rest.

It certainly appeared to, but as he devoted most of his attention to Lydia during the next two hours, Sari began feeling strangely hurt and neglected. She couldn't explain the niggling pain that gripped her as she saw them laughing together, until she suddenly realised that, despite all her self-warnings, she was very much in danger of falling in love with Frank's boss. She refused to believe the searing emotions which swept over her were indelible, but she knew she had been right in deciding that the less she saw of him the better.

When they left to drive back to Carnford, he commented thoughtfully, 'You were very quiet.'

Tartly she replied, before she could stop herself, 'I thought I'd better not distract you while you were deciding about Lydia.'

Brent shrugged, after one of the brief hesitations she was becoming familiar with, 'It was a good chance.'

'And did you approve?' she asked dryly.

'She's a lovely girl.' As they left the town and the car gathered speed, he slanted Sari a lazy glance. 'If Frank can hold her.'

'Good heavens,' Sari exclaimed, with irritaion she didn't try to conceal, 'what a thing to say when they're not even married yet!'

'Divorce is easy.'

'Divorce?' Sari turned to him, her eyes wide. 'Is that how you would approach marriage? I mean, if you ever found someone you wanted to marry?'

'It's a thought which would comfort me a great deal,' he said grimly.

'Then you can't ever have been in love!' she retorted sharply.

'Sari,' his voice was milder, 'I refuse to argue with someone who doesn't know what she's talking about. You've never been in love either.'

'How—how do you know?' she muttered, while relieved to the tips of her gold open-toed slippers that he hadn't guessed she was well on the way.

'You're much too young.'

Did he really believe that? Or was it rather that he wanted to believe she was in no danger of falling in love with him? He must have realised the kisses they had exchanged had been very potent and would have no desire for any complications. She was someone he might amuse himself with, but that was all. Her cheeks scorching, Sari was grateful, as they sped through the countryside, that the darkness must hide her discomfort.

'I'm twenty—almost,' she said at last.

'A great age!'

Why did he jeer so? 'D-don't you believe in love at all?' she persisted, her great eyes wide and fixed on his face.

'I'd be a fool if I did,' came the uncompromising answer. 'Oh,' he allowed, 'I have friends who believe they've found something and call it that, but I'd prefer to call it by its proper name.'

'You—you mean sex?' she said hesitantly.

'Not so naïve, after all, are we, infant?' he laughed, but his laughter had a harsh ring to it which made Sari shiver. 'Compatibility in that direction gets called all kinds of things, and maybe love sounds best.'

'You're a cynic!' Sari said angrily.

'Better that than a disillusioned husband.'

'I suppose you prefer having an affair?' she said, then

was suddenly alarmed by the bitterness she heard in her own voice.

If Brent heard it, he gave no indication.

'It can be safer,' he replied coolly, 'but I dislike ties of any kind.'

She fell silent after that, dwelling moodily on what he had just told her and not knowing what to think. She suspected he was too experienced not to have known a lot of women, and because of this she wasn't sure what to make of his theories. Perhaps she should be grateful to him for revealing that he never took women seriously. If she went on falling in love with him after this, she supposed she could have no one but herself to blame if she finished up with a broken heart.

'You've gone quiet on me again,' Brent smiled, as they arrived home.

'I was thinking,' she said primly.

'I hope about me?' he teased softly, switching off the engine of his powerful Ferrari and turning to her. 'You haven't said if you've enjoyed yourself.'

'I haven't had much chance yet,' she made an effort. 'The meal was lovely, thank you.'

'Only the meal?'

She returned his questioning smile, quite unable to resist it. 'Everything.'

This seemed to please him, but his smile faded as the moonlight caught the sparkling gems at her throat and he bent nearer to hook a finger under them. 'This necklace,' he asked curtly, 'is it yours?'

'Yes.' Sari drew a quick breath, startled and rather frightened at the way his lightest touch sent her pulse racing.

'Where did you get it?'

The abruptness of his query did nothing to soothe her. She remembered his cutting remark when she had said she and Frank were orphans and how hurt she had felt. She didn't know why he should be able to hurt her so easily but rather than expose herself to his cynicism again, by telling him the necklace had been left to her, she replied lightly. 'It was a present.'

'One you should take good care of,' he said tightly. 'It's valuable.'

'Yes.' She wondered why he should be so certain when it might easily have been a fake. She had only her aunt's word that it wasn't, but she didn't want to argue. Something about the necklace appeared to be arousing Brent's anger, and she tried hastily to divert him. 'Shall we go in now?' she asked in a small, hesitant voice, 'I can make some coffee if you like?'

'So anxious to escape?' he laughed, his anger fading as, before she could move, he bent nearer and found her lips. It was a long, sensuous kiss with his knuckles still hard against her throat.

'Don't!' she gasped, as the first hard pressure of his mouth eased enough to allow her to breathe.

'Why not,' he murmured, his voice low, 'when we both enjoy it?' His hand slid from her throat to linger on her full breasts so persuasively she quivered.

'Enjoying something doesn't necessarily mean it's good for you,' Sari replied in a strangled whisper.

She had hoped he might find her answer discouraging, but if anything it appeared to amuse him. 'You're very lovely,' ignoring what she said, his eyes smouldered as he followed the caressing movements of his fingers. 'No wonder Santo . . .' he stopped abruptly.

'What about Santo?' she asked unsteadily.

'Nothing,' he murmered against her hair. 'It was just a remark he made, nothing to alarm you. Forget about Santo. I'd like us to be friends, Sari.'

She dismissed the suaveness she thought she heard in his voice as purely her imagination and suddenly felt happier than she had done all day. 'I'd like that too,' she glanced up at him, her eyes shining, her lips sweetly curved.

She heard him draw a sharp breath as her eyes met his, but before he could say more headlights swept into the drive behind them, lightening the interior of the car.

'Who said the country was quiet?' Brent exclaimed, putting Sari away from him.

'I can't think who it can be at this time of night,' she frowned.

'It's your brother,' said Brent as Frank drove past them. 'Home early, like a good boy.'

'Lydia's working,' Frank explained as they joined him, almost as if he'd heard Brent's mocking remark, but it wasn't Lydia he appeared to have on his mind as he glanced from Brent to Sari sharply, as they entered the house.

Sari wondered if he had noticed her in Brent's arms as he had come slowly along the drive. That seemed the most likely explanation for the grimness of his expression. Yet he had never looked so anxious when she had been out with Santo.

If Brent was conscious of Frank's faint stiffness, he took no notice. The drawing-room was still warm, and she left them talking there while she went and made coffee. When it was ready she put it on a tray with cream and sugar and a plate of biscuits. After carrying it through she said she was tired and thought she would go straight to bed. She didn't look at Brent as Frank nodded, but she was aware of his hooded glance following her enigmatically as she went out.

The next morning Lydia rang.

'Is that you, Sari?' she asked, when Sari went to the telephone. 'I hoped it would be. Is it all right if I come to tea?'

'You know we love seeing you any time,' Sari replied, slightly bewildered, 'but why ask me? You haven't fallen out with Frank, have you?'

'Of course not, silly!' Lydia laughed. 'But he was rather prickly last night when I suggested it. I do believe he's jealous.'

'Jealous?' Sari hadn't a clue what Lydia was talking about. She had plenty of male colleagues and friends, but that never seemed to bother Frank unduly. So why should he suddenly be jealous?

'Of Brent Holding, of course!' Lydia giggled along the line. 'I happened to mention that I thought he was dishy and Frank froze like an icicle—said he was going to be busy this afternoon, and it would be better if I stayed away. That's why I'm asking you.'

Sari didn't know why Lydia's remark should make her feel cold too. 'You know as far as I'm concerned you're welcome any time,' she said sincerely, 'but I don't want Frank to think I'm encouraging you to look at other men.'

'That's all I want to do, love,' Lydia laughed. 'Men really are the limit, as one of these days you're bound to discover. They like looking at other women, but heaven help us if they catch us so much as glancing at other men!'

'I'll tell Frank you're coming.'

'Tell him you persuaded me to change my mind. Anyway, I do want to talk to him about something special.'

Sari hung up after Lydia rang off and went to find Frank. 'Lydia's coming to tea.'

He was working in the office, which he didn't usually do on Sundays. When Sari spoke to him from the doorway, he barely paused to ask why.

'I—I thought it might help,' she said awkwardly.

He still didn't look too pleased. 'Help what, for heaven's sake?'

'Help you stay here, of course,' she exclaimed, wondering why she hadn't thought of it before herself. Surely Frank wouldn't allow jealousy to blind him to the advantages of Brent's approval over his choice of a wife? True, Brent had already met Lydia, but another meeting couldn't do any harm.

'Oh, that?' Frank was amazingly casual, considering what was at stake. 'We've almost everything sorted out—Brent and I, that is.'

'So I understand,' Sari said soberly and with mild exasperation, 'but you can't know for sure what the outcome's going to be, and every little helps.'

'Well, I'd rather fight my own battles, without the assistance of the two women in my life,' he retorted dryly.

When she continued looking at him anxiously, he flung down his pen with a sigh and came round to her side. Putting an arm affectionately around her shoulders, he gave her a little hug. 'Stop worrying, Sari. I guess I'll survive, but how about you? You aren't getting too fond of my boss, are you?'

'Fond of Brent?' she tried to look surprised, but the unexpectedness of his query shook her. She jerked away from Frank, wondering with alarm how much he had noticed.

Her slightly incredulous tones didn't appear to have been entirely convincing. If anything, his thoughtful frown deepened. 'He's a great deal older than you, love, with a lot more experience, and he doesn't take women seriously.'

'I've told you, don't worry!' she said tensely, hoping she didn't look as cold as she felt. 'I can take care of myself.'

'Can you?' Frank began chewing his lip in a way he always did when he was embarrassed. 'It didn't occur to me, until I saw you together in his car last night, that you might be in any danger.'

'Oh, that!' Sari felt so relieved she even managed to laugh. 'He was just being curious about my necklace—you know, the one I was wearing, the one Mother left me.'

'Oh, I see,' Frank sounded relieved. 'If that was all it was . . .'

'That was all,' she forced herself to go on. 'I know he's very attractive, but I have more sense than to begin imagining he would ever look twice at a girl like me.'

Her somewhat devious answer seemed to satisfy him,

as when she left he was smiling again. She didn't enjoy
deceiving him, but if she had confessed to being in love
with Brent, it would only have made him unhappy. And
surely he had enough worries, at the moment, without
her adding to them by admitting to something she
wasn't even sure of herself.

As she helped Anna prepare lunch, she kept thinking
of what Frank and Lydia had said about Brent. He was
experienced—and dishy, she supposed, and wondered if
that was why he attracted her. How did one tell? Did
the instant surge of feeling which sprang between them
each time they touched have nothing to do with it? It
had been too dark to see properly, last night, when he
had brought her home, and they had been nearly
quarrelling, yet immediately his mouth touched hers
something elemental and devastating had fused them
together almost savagely. If Frank hadn't arrived, the
situation, she knew instinctively, might easily have got
out of hand. As Brent's hard body had pressed
compulsively over hers, she had sensed his sudden,
explosive arousal, which, judging from his smothered
exclamation, he had been far from prepared for.

CHAPTER FOUR

LYDIA arrived at four and they had tea around the fire in the drawing-room. Sari wore a soft green sweater over a matching skirt with high-heeled sandals complementing the fine nylon stockings in which she had clad her long, slender legs. Her clothes weren't expensive, but she had good dress sense and for once hadn't resisted the urge to make the most of it. After applying a little light make-up and brushing her red-gold curls into gleaming order, she thought not even her worst enemy could say she didn't look very nice.

Not once during all the unusual care she had taken had she paused to ask herself why. When such a question presented itself at the back of her mind she ignored it. She didn't often discard her jeans before dinner, but she told herself firmly it was because Lydia was coming to tea and for no other reason. It had nothing to do with Brent Holding.

When she had mentioned Lydia's impending visit to him before lunch, he had raised no objection. While she hadn't expected him to, she had thought he might find some excuse to avoid what he might consider a cosy family gathering. Instead he had merely smiled and asked what time Lydia was coming. She had obviously charmed him, Sari had decided hollowly, as he continued smiling after she told him.

As she poured tea, she noticed, as she had done the previous evening, that he appeared to be enjoying Lydia's company. He had on dark pants with a black shirt and looked disturbingly masculine, something which Lydia appeared to appreciate, as she had scarcely taken her eyes off him since she arrived. As she talked and laughed with Brent, Sari realised the other girl was enjoying herself, and that Frank was aware of it too. She wondered if he was jealous. It had occasionally made her curious that it never seemed to bother him, no matter how many men Lydia worked with.

He did seem to be treating her undisguised liking for Brent rather differently, though. Sari saw a frown cross his face and she wasn't surprised to hear him ask Lydia if she still wanted him to accomany her to her cousin's engagement party, the next weekend.

When Lydia hesitated before saying she thought so, this appeared to annoy him. Sari's eyes widened, as she couldn't remember the last time he had lost his temper.

'You either do or you don't,' he said shortly.

Lydia grinned. 'There's no need to bite my head off! How was I to know you'd made your mind up? You said last night you might not be able to get away.'

Frank flushed slightly. 'A farm isn't the easiest thing to leave. And we have a visitor.' he turned to Brent apologetically. 'I haven't asked yet if you'd mind if I took a couple of days off.'

'Oh,' Lydia glanced at Brent, so blatantly flirtatious that Sari's blood boiled, 'I'm sure Mr Holding—Brent wouldn't mind. It's only a weekend, after all.'

Brent glanced at Sari, a mocking glint in his eye before he returned Lydia's smile lazily. 'I expect to be in London by the middle of the week. Even if I wasn't,' he spoke to Frank dryly, 'I think the farm would survive until you got back. You have good men.'

Frank looked surprised and somehow gratified, while Sari felt peculiar inside. She heard Frank thanking Brent and telling Lydia she could let her relatives know they would be coming to the party, but she was really only conscious of Brent. Staring at him, she wondered rather desperately what Carnford would be like without him. She made no attempt to hide the dismay in her eyes as the knowledge of his impending departure hit her like a blow. It wasn't until Cindy, whom she had been stroking on her knee, objected to her tightening grip by growling that Sari realised what she might be betraying and looked away.

'I thought you intended staying longer?' she queried next morning, as she and Brent drove into town. Frank had asked her to post some letters and do some other things for him, and Brent had insisted on going with her. The evening before she hadn't had an opportunity of asking why he had decided to leave so suddenly as Lydia had stayed on, and, after dinner, despite Lydia's obvious disappointment, he had disappeared into Frank's study to make some phone calls and do some work. He had still been there when Sari had gone to bed and she hadn't dared interrupt him.

'I have a conference in London,' he told her now, without glancing at her pale face. 'It's important that I should be there.'

'Won't you be coming back?'

'That depends.'

She would liked to have asked on what, but somehow her courage failed her. There was no reason why he should come back, he had never pretended to have any great fondness for Carnford, and if he did decide to get rid of Frank he could easily get his agent to do that for him. Men like him could afford to pay someone else to do their dirty work for them!

Painfully she swallowed, wishing bleakly that Brent hadn't been with her. As he was driving she had only her unhappy thoughts to concentrate on. If Frank was dismissed it was unlikely she would ever see Brent again, and that made her increasingly aware of her growing love for him. She might only have another few days, then the rest of her life must be devoted to forgetting him.

Briefly she closed her eyes so he shouldn't see the sudden tears in them, and when she opened them again she was relieved to see they were entering the town. As he drove smoothly through the traffic she wondered if it really was a conference which was taking him back to London. Perhaps, Sari thought dully, it was a woman, a beautiful one, like Gloria de Courcy, whom he couldn't wait to see.

Brent had insisted on taking his own car, and, after parking it, he also insisted on coming along while Sari completed the list of things she had to do for Frank.

She was surprised that he never left her side, but couldn't deny she enjoyed having him there. He waited patiently as she dealt meticulously with each item on her list in turn, but as his gaze made a frequent surveillance of her abundant red-gold curls and taut, slim figure, it was obvious that that was what interested him, much more than her apparent dedication to duty.

Because he never took his eyes off her, Sari soon began feeling a little lightheaded and found it difficult to concentrate. Each time he put his hand under her arm to guide her across the street, she felt her heart tremble. And, as his attentiveness had an increasing affect, she tried not to give way to the temptation of pretending he belonged to her, if only for a few hours.

When she finished, and they were having refreshments in a small, olde-worlde café, famous locally for its good coffee, Brent surprised her by suggesting they should go on somewhere for the remainder of the day.

'So far as I can see, you haven't had any time off since I arrived,' he said firmly, as she began protesting. 'Let's explore the countryside and have a picnic. We passed a good delicatessen. If you wait in the car I'll go back and get something for lunch.'

It wasn't within what powers of resistance Sari had left to continue refusing, and she hastily quelled a further twinge of guilt when she remembered she had promised to help Anna with the ironing. That would always be there, but Brent wouldn't, and she had a sudden consuming desire to make the most of what time she had left.

After taking her to the car, he returned twenty

minutes later with a laden hamper. As everything was wrapped, she failed to recognise anything but the shape of a bottle.

'There looks enough there to feed a dozen!' she exclaimed, her eyes round. 'We'll never manage to eat it all!'

'What we don't eat,' he teased, 'you can have for your cat. I'm sure it will make a nice change from all the mice she's supposed to catch.'

'We do feed her as well, you know,' she retorted indignantly, as he wedged the hamper in the back seat before getting in beside her.

'If you didn't feed her so well,' he said derisively, 'and allow her to sleep it off on your bed, she might begin doing something to justify the extremely comfortable life she appears to lead.'

Sari wasn't sure if this was criticism, but as she wanted to make the most of her day, and was determined not to quarrel with him, she decided to treat it as a joke. 'You're just jealous,' she laughed.

'I am—of her place in your bed,' he replied, the smouldering glitter in his eyes belying the lightness of his tones as he slanted a glance at her before returning his attention to the road.

As Sari rarely left Carnford, she wasn't yet familiar with the Cotswolds. Most of what she knew she had learnt second-hand from Frank. This afternoon, however, she didn't feel too concerned over her lack of knowledge. She was content to sit back and relax and secretly watched Brent as much as the passing countryside.

'Where are we going?' she asked at last, oddly reluctant to break the soothing silence that had fallen between them but anxious for fear he was looking for an entertaining companion.

'I'm not quite sure,' he shrugged, lightly, 'but if we get lost we can always ask a policeman.' When she smiled, he added, 'Do you know this area very well?'

'I'm afraid not.' She looked out the car window at the low Cotswold stone walls. It was hilly country, where sheep and cattle grazed. 'When Santo was staying with us, he said he'd been advised to visit the Worcestershire Beacon and Bredon Hill, but we never got that far.'

Brent's expression hardened and she wished belatedly that she had never mentioned Santo.

'How far did you get?' he asked, so curtly that she was certain he wasn't referring to any jaunts around the countryside she and Santo might have shared.

Still determined not to quarrel, Sari made no reply, and as if Brent too realised the folly of provoking each other, he didn't insist on an answer but pressed his foot sharply on the accelerator instead. As the powerful car responded dangerously, she envied him the opportunity of getting rid of his frustration this way.

As the speedometer shot up she felt anxious, but he was an excellent driver and soon slowed down. His shrug of self-derision didn't exactly explain much, but he appeared calmer. Leaving the M5 near Ashchurch, he took the A435 for a little way before branching off on to minor roads until they reached Bredon village. It was a large, attractive village on the River Avon, with a fourteenth-century tithe barn, but he didn't stop. He drove on until they reached Bredon Hill, about three miles to the north-east.

'We can leave the car,' he said, 'and walk to the summit. I feel like stretching my legs.'

Sari didn't mind what she did, so long as it helped to restore his good humour. She was overwhelmingly eager to please him and felt like a humble supplicant ready to prostrate herself humbly before her lord and master.

Her cheeks flushing at the absurdity of her thoughts, she followed him up the hill, clutching tensely at the rug he had asked her to carry. Brent carried the hamper.

'If I take both,' he had grinned, 'I shouldn't have a

free arm to help you when you need it.'

Fortunately—or unfortunately, Sari couldn't decide which, she managed to reach the top without any assistance. The view from the top exceeded her expectations, making her feel the effort had definitely been worthwhile. It was a clear, sunny day and they could see several counties.

'It's wonderful, isn't it?' she exclaimed in an awed voice. 'Like standing on top of the world.'

'Yes,' Brent agreed absently, but while her eyes enthusiastically explored the far distances, his were on her face.

Presently he spread the rug and she sat down by his side as he opened the hamper. She felt like a child watching a mysterious parcel being opened and forgot to hide her air of expectancy. She laughed and said it reminded her of an Aladdin's cave!

Her excitement appeared to amuse Brent. 'I hope I've brought the things you like.'

'I'm so hungry I could eat anything,' she laughed, 'but this is a feast!'

'I think we deserve something after climbing all the way up here,' he quipped.

Sari noticed enviously that, while she was slightly breathless, his breathing hadn't changed. He was remarkably fit, and this puzzled her, as Santo had once told her his uncle spent most of his time in his office. The superb condition of his hard, well muscled body seemed to suggest he took enough exercise of some kind.

They shared the wine and ate chunks of fresh bread with some very good cheese and delicious cold sausages. In the bottom of the hamper was a rich fruit cake and fresh fruit and pots of yoghurt.

'I'm very fond of yoghurt,' Sari sighed, after sampling the fruit cake and a peach, 'but I'm full up.'

Brent laughed, reaching lazily to scoop a trickle of peach juice from the side of her mouth and transfer it to his own. 'I'm glad I've managed to please you.'

Something totally sensuous in what he did made her shiver and the smile slid helplessly from her glowing face. 'The—the food was lovely, thank you,' she stammered.

To avoid the glitter of Brent's grey eyes, she lay back on the rug, pretending a great interest in the sky. After a few moments he lay down beside her and though quite near he wasn't touching. Amazingly Sari began to relax. She began feeling wonderfully happy and peaceful, even drowsy. During the summer she believed a great many tourists came to the area, but today she and Brent seemed to have it to themselves. And, while it might be autumn, the air was still warm, although later in the afternoon it would naturally grow cooler.

Brent was resting his head in his hands and she heard him begin quoting softly. 'Here on a Sunday morning my love and I would lie, And see the coloured counties and hear the larks so high . . .'

'Hush!' she interrupted quickly.

'You aren't a Housman fan, I take it?' He glanced at her sideways, quirking an amused eyebrow.

'I am, but that particular poem has a sad ending,' she faltered, avoiding his gaze.

'Yes,' he agreed more sombrely, 'I believe it has.'

She slept a little after this, reluctant to dwell on endings of any kind, and when she woke it was to find Brent propped on one elbow, studying her closely.

'Time to go,' he said huskily, as her dazed eyes met his and widened.

'Yes,' she whispered, still drowning in his dark, searching glance, 'I suppose it is.'

'You don't sound in a hurry.' His voice slurred on the teasing note he began with.

'I should be!' She tried to speak lightly, but failed as badly as he did.

'Why worry?' He bent his head and his mouth moved against her hair as his arms went round her.

Sari began to speak, although she could never

remember afterwards what she had been going to say. She had wanted to protest, but as soon as she opened her mouth the flames springing up inside her began consuming her. When, with a thickening exclamation, Brent began kissing her passionately, she was lost beyond recall. Her senses went spinning and she let herself surrender entirely to his demands as he crushed her slender body savagely closer.

She had no defence against the hungry urgency of his kisses, and the overpowering strength of his arms made mockery of her feeble struggles. She had had no time to accumulate enough experience to successfully counter his, and her initial defiance died with her last inclination to resist him. Her newly awakened emotions were only capable of responding with a wholehearted lack of pretence. If she had shouted, 'I love you,' from Bredon Hill, at the top of her voice, she couldn't have told him anything her traitorous response wasn't already telling him loudly and clearly.

As if he was getting the message very definitely, he stirred uneasily. Yet, as though he wasn't entirely convinced, he didn't release her immediately. He lifted his head but let his mouth wander over her cheeks and ear, to nibble erotically on her slender neck.

'Do you care for me, Sari?' he murmured softly.

'I love you,' she whispered, her heart beating so fast, it might have betrayed the truth even if she had tried to avoid it.

'You're sure?'

To her surprise his hand raked her hair and he tilted her face for his narrow-eyed surveillance. Her mouth shook as his glittering gaze seemed to probe her very soul. 'Yes,' she confirmed weakly.

Closing her eyes tightly, she tried in vain to find a long, cool breath. Her throat ached and she trembled under the force of passion he had so easily aroused. With each passing moment she expected to hear Brent confess that he loved her too. Surely his kisses and queries must mean he had some feeling for her?

Sari waited fruitlessly, but it wasn't until the silence began penetrating uncomfortably that she opened her eyes again to gaze at him anxiously. 'Brent,' she breathed, 'is something wrong?'

'No,' he said tersely. 'Why should there be?'

As his hands left her abruptly, she flushed painfully. He didn't look like a man in love. His mouth was taut while his eyes glittered too coldly. The coldness in them chilled her hot skin. 'You—you don't love me?'

'No, Sari,' a muscle in his jaw jerked, obviously causing him to pause, but when he continued it was still on a note of cruel indifference, 'I'm fond of you, but that's all. Maybe one day—who knows . . .?'

His voice trailed off uncharacteristically, and, because her eyes were fixed on his face, she saw he was pale. Probably, she thought bitterly, as the extent of her folly washed over her humiliatingly, he was pale because he feared she might embarrass him.

She knew she would never do this, but briefly she felt terribly angry. 'That doesn't explain why you asked if I loved you!'

He rose in one lithe movement, turning from her white accusing face to stare at the view. 'I apologise,'

Just that! Blindly, Sari gazed at the broad back presented to her and wondered if she would ever be happy again? Frantically she tried to control the tears which threatened to fall by scraping together what was left of her pride.

'I'm sorry too,' she said stiffly. 'I don't usually get so carried away. That wine must have been very potent.'

When he swung back to her, she fancied she could actually see the relief in his eyes, and although she knew an uncivilised desire to scream at him, she merely lifted her chin a little higher.

'Would you like to go home now?' he asked hesitantly, as though not quite sure what to make of her new attitude towards him.

'Yes, I would!' She jumped to her feet. Again tears threatened, but she swallowed them. 'It must be getting late. I shouldn't have fallen asleep. Frank and Anna will be wondering where we are.'

'I rang Frank on my way to the delicatessen.'

'Oh, good. I forgot . . .'

They gathered up the remains of the picnic, wrapping the scraps separately and putting everything back in the hamper.

'Still enough for Cindy,' said Brent, his voice curiously expressionless.

'Yes, she'll enjoy it.' A tear fell on his hand and she stared at it, wondering, in hysterical horror, if he would treat it as he had done the peach juice.

'For God's sake!' he exclaimed, startling her. The words seemed torn out of him and before she could move he took hold of her. 'Sari,' he gritted, 'I realise you're mad at me, but I can't be the only man who's kissed you, and you didn't exactly push me away.'

'I'm not mad at you!' She hoped the sudden chill in the air would account for her chattering teeth. 'If anything, I'm mad at myself, but I'd rather not talk about it—please!'

Still he didn't let go of her and his breathing was audible as his arms tightened. Staring down on her, he watched the light hilltop breeze teasing through her gleaming hair, lifting it from her slender neck, blazing it about her small, proud head. His voice was husky as his fingers raised her softly rounded chin and he looked straight in her eyes. 'You're very beautiful—and kissable, you know.'

His mouth lowered to brush her lips. She saw his lips part, the anticipatory dampness of them, and wild sensations shot through her which she tried desperately to fight. Terrified of what more she might betray, she twisted away, wrenching aside her head, driven half crazy with pain. 'Don't!' she moaned.

Brent's hands fell to his sides. He picked up the

hamper and started walking from her, down the hill.

Sari put shaking hands over her face. It was the first time in her life she had ever felt like this and she prayed she would never do so again. The intensity of feeling she had experienced had shaken her to the very core of her being. She still trembled from the explosive mixture of fear and passion she had known in Brent's arms. She had thought his harsh rejection of her love must have cured her of wanting him, but his last embrace had demonstrated frighteningly that this was not so.

If there was anything to be grateful for, it was that he hadn't gone as far as he might have done. Sari was inexperienced, but she knew her body must have been giving out unmistakable signs of encouragement. If Brent had answered all her frantic come-on signals and carried their lovemaking to its natural conclusion, how would she have been feeling now? A whole lot worse, undoubtedly, she acknowledged with a convulsive sob as she wearily followed him down the grassy path to the car.

He was waiting in the car, the engine already running when she slid in beside him, and he didn't look at her as he drove off. When she eventually glanced at him, she noticed his face was oddly flushed and he was gazing at the passing countryside as though totally absorbed. Yet was he really seeing anything? Something in his attitude jerked her eyes curiously back to him after she had looked away again. She could see the red blood creeping over his iron jaw, as if he sought for a control which unaccountably evaded him. His hands were clenched around the steering-wheel, the knuckles gleaming white, and as Sari's puzzled eyes wandered over him, she saw his leg muscles were just as rigid.

Her mind veering slightly, she recalled how those same legs had felt pressing against her own. She had sensed that he knew exactly how to use them in perfect co-ordination with the rest of his body, but he was a man who would enjoy the pleasure his senses could give him just as long as he wasn't dominated by them. As long as his mind was in supreme command, the sensuous side of his nature would be allowed as much licence as it took to satisfy it. But he wouldn't like it, Sari suspected bitterly, should he believe this control was in danger of slipping for even a minute.

How many women, she wondered dully, had he made love to and walked away from while still grappling with the business problem which had probably occupied him all the time he had been giving the impression of undying devotion?

They had almost reached Carnford when he said heavily, 'I hope we can still be friends, Sari.'

Sari started. They hadn't spoken since leaving Bredon and she'd been sunk in unhappy thoughts. Thinking of Frank, she suppressed a sharp retort and nodded numbly. 'Why not?'

'Do you have to be so flippant?' he muttered harshly.

'Does it matter?' she didn't look at him. 'After you go back to London, I don't suppose we shall meet again.'

'You can't know that!' he retorted impatiently. 'It's a small world.'

'Yes, it is,' she agreed, not really aware of what she said, only longing for the sanctuary of her room before giving way completely to the waves of despair which were washing over her. She never wanted to see Brent again—she wished desperately that she had never met him! But as no useful purpose might be served by telling him this, she remained silent. Perhaps much of her heartache was her own fault. If she had been brave and stayed in London with her cousin, nothing she suffered there might have made her feel half as bad as she felt now.

Brent left Carnford next morning. Sari was reluctant to be there to see him off, but Frank especially requested it, and she couldn't find a suitable excuse to avoid doing as he asked. She feared the stoic calm she had managed to preserve during dinner the night before might let her down, but it didn't. Her luck held and she was saved from all but the briefest of farewells by the ringing of the telephone.

Just as Brent gripped her hand, it rang loudly. Swiftly Sari released her numbed fingers from a contact he seemed determined to prolong and gasped to Frank that she would get it. The last thing she remembered was the smouldering darkness of Brent's eyes and the harsh mockery in his voice as he called something after her.

Frank sought her out after Brent had gone. 'Who was that on the phone?' he asked.

'Lydia, but she said it wasn't important and she'd call you back.'

'Which means she doesn't want to be interrupted, whatever she's doing right now,' he smiled wryly. 'I expect it's only about the weekend.'

'She's very excited about it.' Sari gazed at Frank reproachfully, wishing he would at least pretend to be a little more romantic. Still, she reflected, how could she know what he was like when he and Lydia were alone? The prosaic attitude he presented to the world in general might merely be a blind. Take Brent, for instance. Few might ever guess he was ever anything else but a hardheaded business man. His eyes had been glittering coldly as she had left him, and his mouth so tightly held that every hint of sensuousness had disappeared.

'It's going to be quiet without Brent,' Frank said abruptly, watching Sari, suddenly closely. 'He left a bit suddenly, but then he's like that. The first time he came, he just blew in and then was gone. I felt I'd been hit by an avalanche!'

Sari sighed, her face paling. Frank approached like an elephant! Was he throwing out probes, or sympathy? How much had he guessed? 'You might miss him,' she said pointedly, 'but it will be nice to have the house to ourselves again.'

Frank glanced at her quickly, then gave up all pretence. 'You've fallen for him, haven't you? In a big way.'

Sari swallowed, her first instinct being to deny that there was any truth in Frank's allegations. Then she remembered he was her brother and had often known things about her before she had been aware of them herself. 'How did you guess?' she asked hollowly.

'Put it down to family instinct,' he shrugged, 'and one or two glimpses I had of the expression on your face when you were looking at Brent last night. I'm sorry,' he added anxiously.

'It wasn't your fault.'

'No,' he frowned, 'but remarks like that don't make me feel any better. When I first suspected what might happen, I should have sent you away. I should have sent you away before he arrived!'

'We didn't even know he was coming.'

Frank sighed. 'Why doesn't my intuition work as well with other people as it does with you? I didn't think he would. I know profits are down, but I'd just received a substantial rise.'

This brought Sari's mind to her brother's problems again. 'Have you any idea yet if he's going to sell Carnford or let you stay?'

Frank ran his fingers through his hair absently. 'He hasn't said anything about selling Carnford, but it's you I'm worried about.'

'Please don't,' she said, too quickly. 'I—I was bound to develop an infatuation for someone . . .'

'But it's not just an infatuation, is it?' he rejoined tersely, well able to judge correctly the haunted agony in Sari's green eyes.

Sari's slim white hands clenched. She hadn't thought Frank so observant. Bleakly she shook her head. 'But you have to give me a chance, Frank. In time I'm sure to get over it.'

'Perhaps,' Frank worried, 'you need a break. Oh, I

know,' he held up a hand as she began to protest, 'you think you don't need one, but after Aunt Joan died you went straight to London, and, as far as I can make out, tramped the streets from the moment you arrived there, looking for work. And since I brought you to Carnford, you've never stopped working.'

Sari hesitated. She didn't believe it was work which was at the root of her troubles, not altogether. When Aunt Joan died she had been tired, but being young and resilient had been fast getting over it when Brent arrived. It was easier to blame work, though, and not so humiliating.

She said quickly and quite truthfully, 'I've been thinking of going back to Cornwall, to sort out the cottage. As you say, I practically just locked the door after Aunt Joan died. Somehow I couldn't bear to stay. Everything seemed exactly the same, yet so different ...' Her voice trailed off as she wondered if Frank could understand.

He did. 'I'm sorry, love,' his eyes were full of remorse as they rested on her strained face, 'I knew it wasn't easy for you, if I never guessed it was as bad. I had so much on my mind here ...'

'I know.' Her smile was wholly forgiving.

'So you believe you should go back and perhaps decide what's to be done with the place?'

Sari heard the unease in his voice and knew he still didn't like the idea of her being anywhere on her own. While her heart warmed to him, she had to be practical.

'The cottage was left to you, Frank, so you'll have to decide about selling it, but we can't leave it standing empty much longer. Mrs Barrie, down the road, promised to look in and open the windows, but it was only a temporary arrangement. We couldn't ask her to do it for ever. I have to go back some time.'

Frank appeared to accept this. 'When were you thinking of going? If you feel you must, the year's getting on. I shouldn't leave it much later, if I were you.'

'I won't,' she promised.

'Right,' he kissed her cheek awkwardly, 'that's more or less settled, then. And if there's anything I can do, love, either about the cottage or—this other thing, you know you've only to ask. Brent won't be the easiest of men to forget.'

That must be the understatement of the year, Sari thought hollowly, during the days which followed, as she remembered him all the time. Anna asked her to strip his bed, and she felt her legs go weak as she entered his suite and saw the indentation of his head still on the pillow. Had he left it there on purpose, intentionally to remind her of him? Could any man be that cruel? She stood there frowning, her hands stuck firmly down the seat of her slacks to prevent them touching and caressing the place where his head had lain.

Then suddenly her control went and she flung herself on the bed, convulsively clutching the pillow, imagining feverishly that he was beside her. Closing her eyes tightly, she could feel his hard body pressing closer, as it had done on Bredon Hill, feel his mouth hovering before descending slowly. With a moan she turned on her back, raised urgent arms to clasp round his neck, her lips parting, ready to return his kisses passionately but finding only empty space and fresh air.

With a strangled cry of horror directed against herself, she sat up. Was she going crazy? With a jerky sob she slid from the bed and began stripping it. If Anna had caught her, she would also have questioned her sanity. It had been an insane thing to do, falling in love with a man who had merely been amusing himself, but there was no reason to let the world know the depth of misery to which she had sunk.

While she adhered to this line of thought, Sari soon discovered, the anger it aroused helped her to survive as well as anything. Nights were the worst. After two she still wasn't able to sleep properly. The moon was full and it shone through her bedroom window, its romantic beauty, stirring her senses, secretly tormenting her. She didn't even derive any comfort from Cindy's sympathetic purrings at the bottom of her bed and the dark hours stretched interminably.

Then, on Thursday, Santo rang.

CHAPTER FIVE

SARI dropped the newspaper she was busy reading and ran to the hall when the telephone rang. It would be someone for Frank, it usually was. Picking up the receiver, she gave their number.

'Sari?' a masculine voice asked eagerly. 'Is that you?'

Sari paled, for a moment thinking it was Brent, until she realised Brent's voice was deeper. Yet there was a faint similarity. 'It—it's not Santo, is it?' she asked, after confirming her own identity.

'Of course!' he sounded disgruntled. 'I thought you would recognise me immediately.'

'Well,' Sari felt rather at loss for words, 'you're the last person I expected to hear from . . .'

'Why?'

This time she thought he sounded belligerent, but it might be the line. 'Santo,' she asked hastily, 'where are you?'

'In Italy. *Buona sera!*' he laughed dryly. 'With my grandmother.'

'Oh—Brent didn't say.'

'Brent? You've been talking to him?'

'D-didn't you know?' Sari was stammering again, as she often did when she was confused. 'Your uncle's been staying here.'

'Has he indeed!'

Sari gulped, staring at the phone. Santo couldn't be snarling! 'Santo,' she breathed, 'what is it you want? This call must be costing a fortune!'

'It doesn't matter,' he replied impatiently. 'Are you still considering marrying me, Sari?'

'Marrying you. . .?' her voice squeaked, then faded altogether. She had hoped he would have forgotten all

77

that nonsense. And it wasn't as if she had ever taken him seriously.

'You've changed your mind?' Her startled silence appeared to alarm him. 'What's Brent been saying to you?'

'Don't be silly!' she gasped, her mind whirling. 'He knows nothing about it.'

'So you didn't tell him?'

'Just as a—a sort of joke,' she faltered unhappily, 'but I didn't take you seriously.'

'Then you'd better begin to,' he said huffily. 'I'll ring you later and I want to hear you say yes. I'll be home as soon as I can get. Brent said my grandmother was sick, but she isn't getting any worse. Or better,' his voice hardened suspiciously. 'I won't be made a fool of, Sari, by you or Brent or anyone! I'll ring you back.'

Oh, lord! Sari sat down, her head in her hands, thankful that Frank was out. She needed time to think what to do. She had spoken the truth when she'd told Santo she hadn't taken his proposal seriously. He had been upset when he had asked her to marry him and she had been sure he would forget all about it. Now, it seemed, she had to find some way of convincing him she had no intention of marrying him, before he did something foolish like coming here to Carnford.

She wondered how she would have felt if Brent had asked her to marry him, and hastily jumped to her feet. She must stop relating him to everything that happened to her. Far better to concentrate on the fact that she wouldn't be seeing him again!

Lydia and Frank decided to begin their weekend on Friday afternoon.

'It's ages since we had any real time together,' Lydia said happily to Sari, as she paid them a flying visit that evening.

Frank looked so happy that Sari felt compelled to say she thought it a wonderful idea. How could she possibly wipe the glow from their faces by warning

Frank of what Brent had said about taking time off? After all, as she had told Brent, Frank hadn't had a holiday this year.

The next day, after they had gone, the house seemed very quiet. Sari commented on this to Anna.

'It's not just Frank,' Anna replied absently, leafing through her TV programmes while they had coffee, 'it's Mr Holding being out of the house too. You can't help noticing he's not here, but then he's a man who will always make his presence felt. And vice versa!'

Sari wished she had kept quiet. Excusing herself quickly, she went to tidy the office. There wouldn't be a lot to do while Frank was away, just routine things like answering the telephone and dealing with the unexpected caller. Not that there would be many of these in two days. Perhaps she should use the short lull Frank's absence would provide to try and decide what to do about the cottage and Santo.

But she still hadn't reached any definite decision about either, when later, in the evening, she received a terrible surprise. She was helping Anna to wash up after dinner when Brent walked in. The front door was open and when he saw Sari's white face he apologised for not knocking.

'I'm sorry if I gave you a fright,' he said. 'I thought you were used to people running in and out.'

Swiftly Sari tore her eyes from his tall, vital figure, the mocking glint in eyes watching her narrowly. She had a feeling he had surprised her deliberately, although she couldn't be sure. 'G-Good evening,' she whispered stiffly.

Anna, for once undisturbed by the threat of imminent disaster, rose to her feet with an alacrity Sari rarely witnessed. 'Have you had dinner, sir?' she asked calmly.

'Yes, on the way.' He was still inspecting Sari. 'I shouldn't mind a cup of coffee, though. Is Frank about?'

'No,' both Sari and Anna spoke at once, and as Sari paused in confusion, Anna suggested quickly, 'You might like to take Mr Holding to the drawing-room, Sari, and explain, while I make some coffee.'

Sari, never feeling less like explaining anything in her life, gritted her small teeth painfully and obeyed. As she left the kitchen, she was conscious of Brent following her relentlessly, disturbing her rather desperate attempts to find a suitable and plausible explanation as to why Frank wasn't here.

In the drawing-room she gave up and let it all come out in an apprehensive rush. 'Frank and Lydia have gone to a—the party. You knew about it . . .'

'Ah, yes.' Brent stood so pointedly, she had to sit down. He waited until she did so, then took the chair opposite. 'I'm afraid I must have made a mistake,' he drawled suavely. 'I thought they weren't going until tomorrow.'

'I—I believe they decided it would be too great a rush,' she gulped. 'You—you know how it is? If they hadn't left until tomorrow—in the morning, that is, it would have taken them all day to get there, and that wouldn't be allowing for meals, and perhaps an accident on the way. Why, it can take an hour to even mend a flat tyre!'

'I usually change mine,' he commented.

It took Sari all her time not to scream. Inside she felt she was breaking up. She wished bitterly that she felt half as cool as Brent looked! She was making a fool of herself and they both knew it, yet somehow she was unable to stop. 'If they hadn't travelled until tomorrow they might have been too tired to enjoy the party . . .'

'Sari!' Brent's grim exclamation brought her fevered explanations to a sudden halt. 'Who are you trying to defend, and why?'

'I'm not trying to defend anyone,' she denied hotly, 'but you told me you thought Frank took too much time off, and he isn't here to speak for himself.'

'You're doing a good job,' he noted dryly, ignoring her reference to anything he might have said in the past, 'but sometimes it's more convincing to say too little than too much.'

Sari moistened her lips, his advice on diplomacy coming too late. 'He had no idea you would be coming back—at least, not so soon. You should let us know, instead of descending out of the blue as you do! It's not fair to play such a cat-and-mouse game.'

'I don't play games, Sari,' his grey eyes glittered coldly. 'It's other people who do that, and some play for high stakes.'

It seemed to Sari that his contempt was directed against herself and she frowned. 'I'm afraid I don't follow . . .'

'No? Well, think about it.'

Sari moved her feet restlessly, staring blankly down at them. Not for the first time she wished she was more sophisticated. If she had been she might have been able to understand what he was talking about?

She felt relieved when, at that moment, Anna came in with the coffee tray and a pile of freshly cut sandwiches. There was a large hunk of stilton, a bottle of brandy and some biscuits.

Placing it on a low table before Brent, she smiled as he thanked her and asked, 'Shall I make up your bed, sir?'

'That's a good idea, Anna,' he nodded. 'I'll be glad of it, after I've had this and stretched my legs.'

'You're staying?' Sari asked uneasily, after Anna departed.

'I may as well.' Taking charge of the coffee, he poured two cups, catching the dismay in her eyes as he passed her one. His mouth quirked. 'If it's convenient, of course. Now that I'm here I may as well wait until Frank returns. I hadn't anything specially planned for this weekend.'

'There's nothing I can do?' Sari asked hesitantly, not

certain that she wanted to hear him say there was. The thought of having him to herself for a whole weekend was tempting, but she didn't want him to guess she still loved him. And, even if he didn't, wouldn't two or three days in his company act like a dangerous drug? Temporarily it might lift her to blissful heights, but after he had gone she might feel worse than ever. Yet he was Frank's boss, and she wasn't in a position to refuse to let him stay in what was, after all, his own house. He had asked if it was convenient, but she doubted if a negative answer on her part would alter a decision he had obviously already made.

As he shook his head at her halting query, she suggested more swiftly, 'You might be bored.'

'If you hadn't been here I might have been.' As she stared at him apprehensively, he smiled, a smile which startled her.

Sari wasn't sure why it should make her heart tremble, but it was slightly different from the rather caustic ones Brent had occasionally bent on her in the past. His eyes were suddenly kinder and there was a warmth about him that made her breath catch tremulously in her throat.

While he drank his coffee and brandy, she couldn't help stealing furtive glances at his ruggedly good-looking face. She was rather puzzled that he should be wearing what she took to be a business suit. It gave the impression that he had left London on impulse and in a hurry. The dark grey trousers and jacket were beautifully cut but sober, and the matching waistcoat was buttoned tightly over his broad chest. She saw how well the jacket fitted the breadth of his shoulders and was startled when he suddenly threw it off. Then, with quick, impatient fingers, he loosened his tie and the top two buttons of his shirt. As he revealed a strong throat with a sprinkling of dark hairs, Sari's eyes widened and she flushed.

'Won't you be cold?' she searched hastily for a way of

removing his thoughtful attention from her hot cheeks. 'It's not very warm in here.'

'No, I've been wearing this suit all day,' he shrugged, confirming her suspicions. 'I didn't stop to change and I can have a bath later. I suppose we could always light a fire?' he glanced at the well preserved Adam fireplace. 'I see one's already laid.'

'Let me do it.' Sari jumped up to forestall him as he reached for a box of matches, anxious to do anything which might subdue the effect all that potent masculinity was having on her, but he waved her back to her chair.

'You get on with your coffee,' he commanded, his voice surprisingly gentle. 'You've scarcely touched it, or your brandy, and you look as though you could do with both.'

Next morning, although Sari rose early, she was disappointed to discover Brent had beaten her to it. As she ran downstairs she found him coming in at the front door. He was looking less tired than he had done the night before, but his eyes still held a curious strain.

'Hello,' he greeted her softly, his glance going swiftly over her slim young figure. 'You look like an angel descending a heavenly stairway in the sky.'

'Only I don't suppose angels wear jeans,' she laughed, lightly, but feeling absurdly pleased at his compliment.

'You never know what God allows these days,' he smiled, to her utter astonishment dropping a warm kiss on her quivering lips.

'Ha-have you been far?' she stammered.

Mockery twinkled in his eyes as she stepped hastily back, but he didn't look annoyed. 'I think I've walked miles,' he admitted ruefully. 'I had a lot of energy I had to get rid of somehow.' His gaze suddenly altered, becoming more intimate, so Sari knew without words what he would like to have done with it.

As she coloured wildly, he smiled wickedly but took pity on her. 'Is that bacon and eggs I can smell? I could certainly do with some. All that fresh air has given me an appetite.'

After breakfast they took the horses and went riding, and Sari felt it was like the continuation of a dream. If she wasn't quite sure what to make of it, she didn't spend a lot of time trying. Brent was being nice to her. Whereas, before, he had treated her with a certain amount of indifference, both last night and this morning his attitude seemed subtly to have changed. He was more attentive—she still thrilled to remember how nice he had been after supper. They had talked a long time and laughed a lot too, but he hadn't tried to get closer. It was only as he had said goodnight to her, outside her bedroom door, that she had had a definite feeling he would liked to have kissed her.

He had kissed her this morning, though. With a warm feeling in her heart, Sari imagined she could still feel his tender caress, and somehow this curiously passionless kiss more than compensated for the one she hadn't received outside her bedroom. It made her realise, as they rode over the gold-tinted fields, that without love passion alone must provide a peculiarly empty kind of fulfilment. Yet without Brent she knew her life would become quite empty. He would never marry her, Santo had said he would never marry, but she suspected he didn't live like a monk. Would she, Sari wondered, have the strength to resist, should he ever suggest they had an affair? She could be wrong, but he seemed intent, this weekend, on making sure she was aware he felt something for her. Was that what he had in mind?

Yet, when he caught her hand and held it as the horses walked side by side up a steep incline, she didn't think so. He might look slightly wary, but there was a tenderness in his smile which made her pulse miss a beat and her eyes glow. She didn't think any man would even glance at a girl, as he was doing, if he wasn't beginning to care for her, and she decided to stop worrying about the future and let Brent take care of it.

When they returned to the farm he pulled her against him in the dusky half-light of the stables. 'You're very sweet.' His voice had an unexpectedly husky note as he kissed her gently again. As she responded, a warm shine in her eyes, his breathing deepened and the quality of his kiss changed. She felt his lips harden and begin parting hers, while his hands slid to her hips, drawing her tightly against him.

Heady scents filled Sari's nostrils; the scent of hay and sweating horses, the autumn breeze blowing through the open doorway. Yet nothing seemed as potent as the clean masculinity of the man who held her. He only had to hold her lightly to set all her senses ablaze.

Joe's habit of talking to himself must have warned Brent of his approach. Sari heard nothing as Brent's kisses had her floating in space, and she resented the old man's intrusion even as she welcomed it. As he came to take the horses, she noticed his sharp glance and pushed Brent away hurriedly.

'Anna will have our lunch ready,' she murmured, her cheeks flushing red.

'Good.' Brent let go of her slowly, but although the physical contact was broken, another, invisible one seemed to remain. Sari still felt indescribably close to him as they walked back to the house.

'We could go out for dinner again, as we did last week,' he suggested. 'How would you like that?'

She smiled, pausing on her way to the kitchen to give Anna a hand. 'I'd love to!' Her eyes lit up, thinking this time there would only be the two of them. 'Are you sure, though?' her smile faded doubtfully. 'You've had a busy week.'

He looked amused. 'How do you know?'

'Well,' she frowned anxiously, 'you had a conference and last night you looked very tired.'

'I'm used to being busy, and feeling tired. But,' his

mouth quirked teasingly, 'remember the old saying about all work and no play——?'

Sari laughed and gave in gracefully, and at lunch didn't bother to try and hide the happiness in her eyes. She couldn't remember ever feeling so happy before. Brent had left Carnford on Tuesday with scarcely more than a brusque goodbye. After the somewhat disastrous ending to their picnic on Bredon Hill, he had dropped all pretence of friendship and returned to being an autocratic employer. Now, amazingly, he had apparently decided to be friends again. How this had come about she couldn't be sure. She could only conclude that he must have had a change of heart in London and regretted his abrupt departure. She hoped his good mood would last until Frank returned and it might induce him to offer Frank a permanent position, rather than to sack him. As for herself, Sari was suddenly recklessly determined to enjoy the weekend, regardless of its outcome.

After lunch they were interrupted by a group of indignant hikers about a public footpath which they couldn't locate. After studying their map, Sari wasn't sure where it was either, but she offered to take them to consult old Joe, who had lived in the district all his life and considered himself an authority on every inch of it. Brent surprised her by offering to relieve her of the task, and she was quite pleased to allow him to take over.

He had only been gone ten minutes when the telephone rang. Believing it would be Frank, who had promised to get in touch, she didn't bother to reiterate their number but said immediately, 'Hello, Sari here.'

'Oh, good!' exclaimed a voice which certainly wasn't Frank's. It was Santo!

Sari bit her lip in vexation, wishing she had let Anna answer the phone and say she wasn't at home. However, if she had done so, it was more than probable that he would have rung back, so perhaps it might be as well to hear what he had to say and be done with it.

'Hello,' she murmured distantly, hoping to discourage him.

She couldn't have succeeded, because straight away he began aggressively, 'Have you thought any more about marrying me, Sari?'

'Marrying you?' she repeated, her only desire being to slam down the phone and run. 'Oh, Santo!' The despair in her voice heightened it, making her sound oddly breathless, but as before when he had talked of marriage, she felt terribly confused. Marriage, she thought wryly, would solve a lot of her problems, but, although she hated hurting anyone, she knew she could never marry Santo.

'You have thought about it, then?' he asked insistently, as if hoping to force her to a definite decision.

'Yes, oh, yes!' she hastened to assure him.

'Good,' he replied, his tone more impatient than loving. 'I was sure you wouldn't let me down. I'm coming to see you next week, as soon as I return to England.'

'Oh, Santo,' she whispered helplessly, 'must you?'

'Don't you want to see me?' he asked urgently.

Sari gripped the receiver until it hurt. Perhaps it would be better to see him, as she doubted if she would be able to convince him of anything over the phone.

'Yes,' she exclaimed quickly, suddenly making up her mind, 'I'd love to see you, Santo, any time.'

'You'll be at Carnford?'

'I'll be here,' she promised.

'Great!' he laughed exuberantly. 'I don't know how I'm going to wait, darling.'

The endearment shocked her, but she managed a rather strangled goodbye. 'Until next week,' she added hastily as the receiver clattered from her hands.

The shock that eddied through her increased greatly as she turned her head and caught Brent watching her.

Something in his eyes froze her to the spot. He couldn't have been there for more than a minute, she quickly assured herself, and the frightening flash of what she had taken for anger in his eyes might simply have been a trick of the light.

When he smiled gently and stepped inside from the doorway, she knew she had misread the expression on his face. 'Nothing urgent, I hope?'

Guiltily she moved from the telephone which she was startled to find she was trying to hide. 'No,' she hoped he didn't notice the faint colour in her cheeks, 'just someone with the wrong—number.' She had been about to say, 'ideas,' but hastily substituted the other instead.

Making a greater effort to pull herself together, she forced herself to return Brent's smile. 'You soon got rid of the hikers.'

'I left them with Joe.' His voice was faintly reproving but still mild. 'There was nothing more I could do, and he's quite confident he can solve their problem.'

'I see.' That would explain why he had returned so quickly. Glancing at him furtively, she wondered again what it was she couldn't read in his face. Then, pushing her nameless fears aside, she asked, 'Are you ready for coffee?'

'Please.' His eyelids dropped over glittering eyes, but only for a moment. Raising them again, he suggested invitingly, 'How about taking it to the drawing-room and spending a lazy afternoon, before preparing for a riotous evening?'

The afternoon was lazy and Sari, after putting Santo determinedly from her thoughts, enjoyed it. They sat before a roaring fire, which they didn't really need, and watched one of Bob Hope's old films on television, then played records while eating one of Anna's famous teas.

Afterwards, Brent insisted that they went for a long walk. 'If I stayed here I'd soon be overweight,' he laughed. 'Anna's worse than my own lot.'

'Do you have a big staff?' It was something Sari hadn't thought of before—where he lived; who looked after him?

'Just enough to see to my needs,' he replied vaguely.

Glancing at his tall figure, well muscled but without an ounce of surplus flesh, Sari was sure it would be a long time before he need worry about it. He obviously took enough exercise of a sufficiently strenuous kind, despite what Santo had once derisively said about his uncle never leaving the office!

She was silent as, for all her efforts, the telephone call she had had from Santo returned to haunt her. She couldn't help feeling she ought to have been more decisive. Next week, when he came, she must make it clear she had no intention of marrying him. If necessary she would enlist Frank's help, but she hoped it wouldn't come to that. She hoped it could all be managed quietly without Brent ever knowing Santo had been here.

'A penny for them?' Brent offered, apparently idly, slanting a sideways glance at her worried frown.

Sari almost jumped with surprise, for she hadn't realised he was taking any notice of her. 'I'm sure they're worth more than that,' she retorted lightly.

'Are they?' His voice was loaded with dry cynicism, and she bit her lip when his shoulders lifted as if to further demonstrate his disbelief that they were. Might he not change his mind, Sari wondered hollowly, if she had chosen to reveal exactly what she had been thinking about?

As they returned home, to her relief he appeared to forget whatever it was that bothered him and reverted to being the charming companion he had been this morning again. He held her hand and again his body, as he drew closer, seemed to be giving off the heady male scent which had so stimulated her senses in the stables after their ride. Much as she tried not to let it, her now escalating imagination fed on what were probably merely friendly, meaningless gestures, and she couldn't entirely control a response that betrayed itself through fingers which began entwining tightly around his.

It was after seven when she showered and started getting ready to go out with him. Her hands trembled and she couldn't understand why she should be feeling so nervous. It wasn't as if this was the first time Brent had taken her out to dinner, and she felt impatient with the confusing flashes of uneasiness which kept stabbing her.

'How do I look?' she asked, half an hour later when she went to Anna's small sitting-room to say goodnight. She was wearing the second of the two long dresses she owned and had bought it only two days ago in Cheltenham. Frank had said there would be several parties and dances which they would be expected to go to during the autumn, and she couldn't turn up in the same dress all the time. The dress she had chosen was far from expensive, but the pale silk lent her slender body a surprising style. With her hair brushed to a dancing, shimmering cloud, she looked startlingly beautiful.

Anna told her so in no uncertain terms. 'You look lovely—and don't be late back.'

Sari was used to Anna putting everything she had to say in one sentence and was turning away when she was startled to hear her add,

'It's maybe a pity Mr Santo wasn't here.'

Sari's eyes widened as she exclaimed, 'Why, Anna, Santo means nothing to me!'

'That's maybe safer than going out with a man who means too much,' Anna muttered cryptically, returning to her supper which, in view of her night off, she had carried to her room on a tray.

'Would you mind explaining yourself?' Sari rounded on her angrily, unable to believe she could have given herself away.

'Would you mind stopping interrupting my programme?' Anna retorted sharply, her eyes fixed in pleasurable anticipation on the TV screen.

How easily a few words could destroy one's confidence, Sari thought bitterly, leaving Anna in peace.

Brent took her to Cheltenham again, as he said he knew it better than any other place in the Cotswolds, having occasionally been to race meetings there. This time they dined in a different restaurant, although equally luxurious. Sari gazed around with interest, noting the elegance of the clientele, and when some of the other diners would have spoken to him, he merely nodded coolly as he had done when he and Sari had been out before, and took no further notice.

While he consulted with the wine waiter she couldn't help noticing how attractive he looked. The thick darkness of his hair was subdued to glossy order, moulding the back of his well shaped head. She knew a great urge to slide her fingers through it, to rumple it to the deep waves it developed when the wind teased it when they were out riding. She liked his dark evening suit and tie, the way his white shirt contrasted effectively with his faintly tanned skin, but while the urban air such an outfit gave him excited her, it also made her feel curiously out of her depth.

She wasn't conscious of the wine waiter's departure until she became aware of Brent's gaze wandering leisurely over her, a faintly mocking glint in his eyes as he took special note of her hairstyle and dress. Her heart lurched a little as she realised he had known of her own close inspection and was daring her to object to his.

His glance hardened as it reached the delicate lines of her neck. 'I see you're wearing—that necklace again.'

'Why shouldn't I?' she asked defiantly, unable to explain that she had been reluctant to, remembering his former dislike of it, but, unadorned, her neck had looked terribly bare and she hadn't had anything else.

'No reason,' he said indifferently, but she shivered at

something indefinable in his eyes, the moment before they released her.

The food was good, the wine excellent, and afterwards they danced. On the dance floor, not a very large space, he held her close, and she felt her body trembling as his nearness began affecting her. The wine she had drunk, though confined to a small measure, began relaxing the wary tension in her limbs, a tension which had kept her on edge throughout dinner, but she still couldn't rid herself entirely of some nameless apprehension.

She wasn't altogether sure of Brent's mood. Earlier she had decided they were both in two, one angry, one curiously in tune with each other. Nothing seemed to make sense, and while she had no desire to become a victim of her senses, the situation was threatening to get beyond her ability to assess it clearly.

His arms tightened their hold on her, one hand coming up over her shoulders behind her nape, finding the gold clasp of her necklace, giving it a little jerk as if he would liked to have taken it off. His fingers burned her sensitive skin, and she visibly panicked yet couldn't draw away from him.

'Did I frighten you?' His hand returned to her waist as his mouth went to her ear.

Again she shivered. 'A little,' she admitted.

'Why?'

'I should be asking you, I think.'

He laughed and she felt his breath feather her cheek. 'I always realised you're smart.'

'I'd never be able to match you!'

This time his laughter seemed infuriatingly complacent. 'Don't sound so bitter, Sari. A lot of men aren't able to do that. And why should you worry, unless you believe I'm a threat—perhaps to some future plans you might have made?'

'I don't make plans,' she retorted stiffly. 'At least, not the devious kind you seem to be hinting at. Unless you mean Frank?' She had forgotten about Frank and found all her apprehension returning.

'I wasn't thinking of Frank,' Brent said tersely, meeting her stare of wide-eyed enquiry, 'nor did I intentionally seek to upset you. I suggest we forget about your brother and everyone else but ourselves. I brought you here to enjoy yourself.'

'Why do we always fight?'

He smiled into her faintly rebellious eyes. 'We don't have to—but you're not suggesting the fault is always on my side?'

Sari was about to protest when he drew her closer again and she quite forgot what she had been going to say as his mouth moved over her cheek in gentle persuasion. How could she not give in to him, she thought blindly, when he chose to influence her in this particular way?

It was midnight when they left, one o'clock when they returned to Carnford. Arriving at the farm, Brent switched off the engine of his car, briefly surveying the outside light left burning by Anna, with the rest of the house swathed in darkness. Then he turned back to look at Sari, in the passenger seat. Their eyes met and clung, a message flashing between them. Then Brent left the car to go round to her side and help her out.

Sari usually hopped out of any vehicle unaided, but for once had a curious desire to be treated as though she were helpless. Brent certainly knew how to do this, but curiously his gentle expertise, instead of making her feel like a piece of Dresden china, as she had expected to, chilled her. She had expected to be filled with pleasure, but the practised confidence of his movements strangely produced the opposite effect.

He made no move to go inside immediately and her heart started to beat unevenly as she raised her head and he dropped a kiss on her enquiring mouth. 'I've wanted to do that for hours,' he murmured, his lips twisting in self-derision. 'In Cheltenham, I confess, I could think of nothing else.'

Sari avoided his intent eyes but knew what he was talking about. All night, each time her gaze had wandered over his strongly hewn features and lingered on the firm outline of his mouth, she had recalled how she had felt in the stables, when he had kissed her, and longed for him to kiss her again. The touch of his lips on her cheek as they had danced had proved an added incitement.

If Joe hadn't interrupted them in the stables, would Brent have drawn her down on the hay? It had been on his mind, because his glance had gone to it. There she might have discovered if he was beginning to feel about her, the same way as she did about him.

But Joe had come, and later in the afternoon, when she had had time to think of it, she had told herself she should have been glad. Yet that didn't explain the peculiar yearning inside her that wouldn't go away and remained, no matter how desperately she tried to ignore it.

CHAPTER SIX

In the darkness Sari swayed towards Brent involuntarily and his arms immediately enclosed her. As he pressed her light weight to the hardness of his body, she tried urgently to obliterate the sudden rush of wild excitement which threatened to consume her.

With a husky apology, for she believed it was she who had initiated the embrace, she tried to push away from him, but her hands only managed to exert a little pressure on his chest when he bent his head to kiss her again.

His mouth stopped brushing hers lightly and hardened to take complete possession, and Sari's hands stilled as the strength went out of her. Frightening flutters of rapture closed her eyes with delight. Her heart contracted as she felt the need inside him expressed through the warmth of his lips.

Then something halted him, she could feel it like invisible brakes. One moment his arms tightened painfully, the next he was easing her away. He was oddly indecisive, reminding her of the twin moods he often appeared to be in. There was no doubt, she decided hollowly, that he desired her, but whether any woman might have aroused his feelings as she was doing, she had no way of knowing.

'Let's go inside,' he muttered, her small shiver apparently convincing him she was cold, thus prompting him to move from their position beside the car.

Sari glanced from the rather tense lines of his face to the stars above them, so distant, yet so evocative in their silent, glittering challenge. Did they ever realise the influence they had on people billions of miles away?

'Yes,' she agreed, and, as his arms dropped to his sides, walked towards the house.

In the hall, he asked softly, 'Will you join me for a drink?' As she hesitated, he pressed his advantage, 'Tomorrow, after Frank comes home, I'll be leaving. This might be the last chance we have of sharing anything.'

Put this way, how could she refuse? In a kind of dream she followed him to the drawing-room, where he stirred the embers of a dying fire.

'What will you have?' Brent threw off his jacket impatiently, laying it across the back of a chair. Then he crossed to the drinks cabinet, which he had generously replenished during his previous visit.

'Nothing. Well, just anything.' Sari withdrew sharply from her trance-like surveillance of his dark head and powerful shoulders, staring instead at the smouldering fire, trying to think straight. There was the clink of a bottle against the side of the cabinet, the bubbling sound of liquid being poured, then the cool stem of a glass was placed in her slim hands as Brent sat down beside her.

'Drink up,' he commanded, his eyes on her creamy pale face. 'You look tired.'

'I am.' She was glad of a convenient excuse for her pallor. 'I'll have this and go to bed.' She didn't want to leave him; she had a wild desire to confess that she would like to stay with him for ever. But she had to go as soon as possible, because she could never risk having him guess.

'Stay a little longer?' He laid a persuasive hand on her arm.

Could she? Her glance swivelled from the strong column of his throat, unwilling to see anything that didn't reassure her. Old inhibitions were hard to cast aside, but might be worth their weight in gold on some occasions. Temptation flared. It might be possible to meet Brent halfway without committing herself completely. It should be possible to survive somehow.

Obediently she said nothing more about retiring and

A compelling love story of mystery and intrigue... conflicts and jealousies... and a forbidden love that threatens to shatter the lives of all involved with the aristocratic Lopez family.

⌐ Mail this card today for your FREE gifts.

TAKE THIS BOOK
AND TOTE BAG FREE!

Mail to: **SUPERROMANCE**
1440 South Priest Drive, Tempe, Arizona 85281

YES, please send me FREE and without any obligation, my **SUPERROMANCE** novel, *Love Beyond Desire*. If you do not hear from me after I have examined my FREE book, please send me the 4 new **SUPERROMANCE** books every month as soon as they come off the press. I understand that I will be billed only $2.50 per book (total $10.00). There are no shipping and handling or any other hidden charges. There is no minimum number of books that I have to purchase. In fact, I may cancel this arrangement at any time. *Love Beyond Desire* and the tote bag are mine to keep as FREE gifts even if I do not buy any additional books.

134-CIS-KAEK

Name	(Please Print)	

Address		Apt. No.

City	

State		Zip

Signature   (If under 18, parent or guardian must sign.)

SUPERROMANCE

EXTRA BONUS
MAIL YOUR ORDER
TODAY AND GET A
FREE TOTE BAG
FROM SUPERROMANCE.

Mail this card today for your FREE gifts.

drank whatever it was he had given her, not because she really wanted it but more to please him.

He drained his glass and asked if she would like another? When she refused he took both their glasses and set them aside. Then he turned to her again, laying his arm along the back of the sofa, behind her, so he was very close.

Something started to jerk at the base of her throat and she put her hand over it, not wanting him to notice her sudden fright. Licking dry lips, she murmured, 'Doesn't the fire need attention?'

'It's the fire inside me that needs that,' he growled mockingly, his glance slanting over her. 'Aren't you going to deal with it?'

Which fire did he mean? She could discover nothing from his silky smile, but felt slightly better when he said soothingly,

'I'm sorry—I promise not to tease you any more.'

She took comfort from this until she found herself drawn swiftly to him. 'No!' she exclaimed, jumping up before his arms could tighten.

'Sari!' He caught her, pulling her back so that she fell halfway over his knees. 'Why?'

Didn't he know? Couldn't he guess? She had been mad to think she could play with him, but it wasn't too late. 'Brent,' she cried, gulping air, 'd-don't touch me!'

It must have been too late. Even as she spoke, her body was melting against him with a will of its own. When he lifted her face she knew she could deny him nothing.

'You want me to touch you,' his eyes fixed on her lips, 'as much as I want you to touch me. You can't help yourself, can you, Sari? You may not think you're leading men on, but you give them enough encouragement, and it's no use panicking when you find one who has you all weighed up.'

Whatever was he talking about? But even as she wondered, his mouth cut a decisive path to hers, stamping an intimate possession. He pulled her to him, his hands crushing and caressing, threatening to stop her breathing. She began struggling, then found herself losing all desire to oppose him. Her heart throbbed with an aching force as her whole body became inflamed under the burning pressure of his kisses. Parting her numbed lips, Brent explored every corner of her bruised mouth, while his hands roamed her slender body. Beneath the sensuous expertise of his kisses, Sari soon trembled with mounting passion.

The wine she had imbibed hadn't affected her like this. Feverishly she clung to him, drunk on the taste of him. There was nothing she could do to prevent her hands searching round his bare throat, seeking the back of his head, clinging so tightly he would have had to be made of stone not to have understood her urgent message. She was drugged by the scent and sound of him, by the soothing things he murmured against her lips and in her ears.

His heart was beating heavily through the thin silk of his shirt and he didn't try and hide it. It seemed to be pounding into her own, bringing her alive as she had never been before. His mouth began making dizzying forays on her cheeks and down her neck, while his hands discovered the taut peaks of her breasts, sending raw shivers of desire coursing right through her.

When he eventually lifted his head she no longer had any clear idea where she was or what she was doing? 'Are you still eager to go to bed?' he murmured thickly.

She heard his voice and vaguely understood, although the exact context of his question escaped her. 'Yes,' she replied quickly, her swimming senses resenting any intrusion.

She was still clinging to him blindly as Brent asked softly, 'Alone?'

How could she bear to let him go? Tomorrow he would be gone. There were only a few more hours! She wanted to be with him as long as possible. Dazedly she shook her head, her breath stolen by the traitorous awakening of feelings she had never guessed she possessed. Overwhelmed by them, she wanted Brent to stay with her for ever.

He must have decided further words were unnecessary as he picked her up immediately and carried her upstairs. Sari didn't remember him taking her to her bedroom. Even in the half-light it must have been difficult for him to find his way, but he never stumbled. She was vaguely conscious of a door closing and of a bed, soft and cool, under her heated limbs. The coolness of the sheets brought a brief awareness of what was happening, but her yielding, treacherous body was filled with such passionate yearning that nothing else really registered.

The only hurt Brent inflicted, to begin with, was when he jerked off her mother's necklace. He removed it so ruthlessly Sari was sure the catch broke, but she forgot it instantly as he turned her over and slid down the zip of her dress. There was a whispering rustle of silk, then he dealt in the same manner with her bra, snapping it open, dragging the straps from her shoulders and throwing it after her dress on the floor.

The pile of clothes that followed must have belonged to them both, but Sari was past caring. Moments later Brent was lying beside her, his mouth burning her into a roaring conflagration. She trembled as he covered her with kisses and she felt him shudder against her. As he moulded her to his hard male body, her desire grew to something she could scarcely contain. Her passion, blinding her to shame, made her try to get even closer to him by wrapping her arms around him and arching herself wantonly against him.

He wasn't gentle, but the fever inside her didn't worry about that. If anything it seemed to welcome his slight cruelty. When his hands began caressing the soft fulness of her breasts until the nipples hardened to meet the demands of his mouth, the frenzy he aroused threatened to drive her out of her mind. But when she whimpered his arms merely tightened and he muttered something unintelligible against the quivering warmth of her skin.

Her hands ran restlessly over his shoulders, and, as she tried to tell him how much she loved him, the breath disappeared from her lungs. Every part of her turned to liquid fire, and when his mouth returned to hers she was too aroused to even manage one word. Her whole body was a vortex of burning desire. She felt so passionately committed that she offered herself completely, believing he would always be kind and never hurt her.

That was where she made her greatest mistake. As the fluid surrender of her body acted like a potent, highly powerful stimulant, Brent's control went and he hurt her unbearably. As he parted her limbs and his hardness invaded her, Sari screamed wildly and began struggling, as she was plunged from the haze of delight she had been in to harsh reality.

For a moment she thought he would let her go and her clenched fists stilled on his sweat-coated shoulders. 'It's too late!' she heard him gasp. 'Oh, God!'

There followed more pain, during which she writhed frantically under him. Then, as she thought she was near fainting, to her surprise another sensation took over. Amazingly most of the hurt disappeared and she found herself reaching towards something that beckoned, incredulously and irresistibly. Brent's mouth was crushing hers while his hands guided and his heavy body promised ecstasy. Then all around came explosions of dazzling light, sweeping her up to unbelievable heights, a sensation which went on and on until her gasping cries mingled with Brent's shuddering groans as he collapsed against her.

Sari didn't know how long it took to return to normality. She felt strange, as though she wanted to cry and go to sleep, both at the same time. Numbly she stirred, but was held down by Brent still lying half on top of her.

Then, with a harsh exclamation, he rolled away, avoiding her pleading hands which wouldn't have let him go. Getting to his feet, he paused by the bedside, staring down at her, the line of his jaw white and tense.

'Brent?' Sari whispered uncertainly, unconscious of the moonlight from the uncurtained window revealing the bewilderment in her eyes.

But there was no tenderness in the glance which surveyed her, no hint of remorse in the scrutiny he bent on her pale face. 'I had no idea you were a virgin,' he said bluntly, 'not until it was too late. If you want an apology I'll give you one, but I imagine you knew what you were inviting.'

'Brent!' This time she gasped his name apprehensively, her green eyes widening with dismay.

Ruthlessly he cut her off. 'I told you I believed you played for high stakes. Unfortunately, this time I think you've lost. I don't want you, and when I tell Santo I had you first, I don't think he will, either. He's half Italian, remember, and Italians rarely marry women who've belonged to other men.'

The dismay in Sari's eyes gave way to horror as he spun from her towards the door.

'Wait!' Her voice rose wildly as she almost fell from the bed, stumbling after him to grasp his arm as he took no notice of her frantic cry. 'Please,' she gulped, as he was forced to halt, 'you can't realise what you're saying! Don't you love me?'

'Love you?' His eyes, glittering over her, reminded her too late of her nakedness, while the contempt in his harsh tones answered her anguished query before he spoke. 'You must be out of your mind!' he said.

'No . . .!' Her strangled protest was full of unbearable distress and savagely he threw off her clinging hands. She stumbled again, this time backwards, and fell against the same high chest on which, when he first came, he had found the snap of her and Santo. Her head caught the edge of it with a bang, but Brent merely glanced at her indifferently.

'I advise you to pull yourself together,' he snapped, making no attempt to assist her, 'or both you and your brother will be out of here fast! Oh, and by the way,' he added coolly, as he left, 'I'm taking the necklace. Santo had no right to give it to you.'

As the door slammed behind him, Sari slumped against the ornate tallboy. Her head hurt yet felt like thick cottonwool, and when she tried to get up everything went black and the room receded. When she regained consciousness she was still on the floor, but she noticed the light had changed. Dawn had arrived, a dull, grey dawn, and she wondered dazedly what she was doing lying on the carpet.

Then, as full realisation hit her, she dragged herself upright. Her legs were so shaky she had to grasp the edge of a chair and she was sure she was going to be sick. She could scarcely bring herself to look at the bed, and when she did she hurried to cover it up. How could she have given herself so completely to a man who didn't love her? While he had never said he did, she had stupidly believed the recent friendliness he had shown must mean he returned her feelings.

Sari shuddered, hate welling in her heart, almost strangling her. Without caring for her in the least, Brent had ruthlessly taken everything which she, in her innocence had offered. Never—she swallowed a sob— would she forgive him, and fiercely she hoped she would never see him again.

The problem of how to avoid him began tormenting her fevered mind. As she dressed she tried to decide the best way to do it. It was Sunday, a day when few buses ran, so she thought it might be better to take the small pick-up and disappear for the day. She found a pad and hastily scribbled a note for Anna, to leave in the kitchen. By the time she returned, Frank would mercifully be back and Brent gone.

It wasn't until she glanced dully in the mirror to see if there were any visible signs of the ordeal she had suffered that she noticed the red mark on her neck. Not until then did she recall Brent taking her necklace and the remarks he had made about it. He obviously believed Santo had given it to her, and she shrank from the prospect of facing him in order get it back. She must just trust that Santo would explain that he had never given her any jewellery of any kind, and Brent would return it.

When she crept downstairs, a few minutes later, trembling with apprehension at the thought of bumping into him, it seemed a terrible anticlimax to discover that he had already gone. He had left a message where she had intended leaving hers, on the kitchen table. Brent's was written on a flat piece of paper, and she read it. He merely said he had decided to return to London and would see Frank another time.

Her face white, Sari stared at it, wondering if the purpose of his visit had had much to do with Frank at all. It seemed he might merely have been using Frank to cloak his real mission. During the last few days, while he had been in London, Brent must have been in touch with Santo, who must have convinced him that he was seriously considering marrying Frank's sister. After which, Brent had come to Carnford with the deliberate intention of putting a stop to such an unsuitable alliance. If the method he had employed had ruined a girl's life, his conscience would never have troubled him, not in view of the results he would believe he had achieved!

Feeling too sick at heart to drive anywhere, especially now that the necessity to do so was removed, Sari went for a ride on Sheba instead. Tearing up her note, she rode to the far corner of the estate. Here, in the loneliness of a stretch of high, uncultivated ground, she flung herself on the grass beneath some trees. She had thought she might find relief in tears, but the tears which eventually escaped her burning eyes scalded her frozen cheeks and were few.

To Sari, it seemed the whole of her was frozen, incapable of movement or even thought of any kind. Shock, which she believed she had managed to get under control, after a rather terrifying half hour of reaction in the bathroom after she had woken up, threatened to overwhelm her again. Only one thought dominated her reeling mind, and that was the need to escape. She felt sure Brent would never return to Carnford, but if he did she couldn't possibly face him. And, apart from that, the need to hide her shame from the world began to obsess her. Other girls might sleep around and think nothing of it, but she had never been able to. And that she had given herself to a man who despised her made her feel even worse. She had to get away, to have time to come to terms with herself again.

Frank returned late that evening after dropping Lydia off at the flat which she shared with another girl. While Anna fussed over him with sandwiches and a huge pot of tea, Sari waited with tense impatience for the housekeeper to retire.

When Anna did, Sari turned to her brother. He had already said how much he had enjoyed his weekend and related brief details. After Anna went, Sari could see he was tolerantly expecting her to ask more questions, and was surprised when, instead, she broached the subject which had occupied her all day.

'I've decided to go to Cornwall tomorrow, Frank. We discussed it before you went away, remember?'

'Yes,' he carefully put down the sandwich he had lifted towards his mouth, after taking a closer look at Sari's face. 'Why the rush, though? If you don't mind my saying so, you look terrible. Sari,' his voice sharpened, 'Anna said Brent's been here. Just what's been going on?'

Sari had a story all ready. She was ashamed of

having it almost off by heart, but Frank, in certain moods, wasn't easy to fool.

'Nothing much,' she actually managed a light shrug. 'Brent came to see you—he didn't say what for, but I imagine he'll be in touch. No,' she swallowed, 'he's not the problem. It's Santo—he rang.'

'Santo?' Frank looked puzzled. 'What on earth did he want?'

'Me,' Sari replied, grateful that she remained so cool. 'He swears he's coming to Carnford this week, and I'd rather not be here when he arrives. He insists he wants to marry me, but I certainly have no wish to marry him. I don't know that I take him seriously either,' she added, as Frank's brows rose incredulously, 'but I don't want to take any risks. That's why I thought it would be easier all round if I just disappeared.'

Frank stared at her in growing amazement. She could see he felt momentarily out of his depth. 'Had you any idea Santo felt this way about you?'

'None. At least,' she confessed unhappily, 'he got a bit hysterical when he said goodbye, but I thought he would soon forget.'

'And he hasn't.'

'Apparently not—but Brent would never approve.'

'You're right there,' Frank's mind veered in the direction Sari hoped it would, 'I can see that.'

'So—all the more reason to avoid anything which might upset him,' Sari laboured on. 'If you're thinking of getting married you can't lose your job—which you might if I become a bone of contention!'

'Well, as I suppose you were going to Cornwall anyway,' Frank pondered, 'it might be for the best . . .'

'As long as you promise not to mention to anyone where I am,' Sari insisted urgently, 'especially not Brent or Santo. Brent would probably come and murder me, just to make sure I was out of the way permanently. And,' her face whitened, 'I would die rather than see him!'

'Sari——' Frank was suddenly a man who was sure

he should know something he didn't, 'there's more than Santo wrong, I can tell!'

'No,!' Sari averted her tormented face, trying to keep her voice under control. 'No,' she repeated with a small, helpless sob, burying her face in her hands. 'But please, Frank, don't ask any more questions.'

There was a grim pause, then he said slowly, 'I'd like to know what the hell's been going on to get you in such a state, but if you won't tell me, you won't. If you're only having a little panic over Santo, I can only say leave him to me. But if anyone's done anything to harm you, heaven help them!'

Feverishly, Sari rubbed her eyes and raised her head again, shaking it emphatically. Frank must never be allowed to guess! 'No,' she whispered, 'I'm just being silly. I think, as you say, I've worried myself into a state of nerves. Perhaps I need a change.'

Faint relief showed in Frank's eyes as he nodded. 'That's my girl! But where will I say you've gone?'

'Oh . . .' Sari blinked anxiously, 'anywhere. No, you'd better make it London. It's big enough, no one would ever find me there. You can always say I'm with Cilla, if you were pushed. She'll probably be out of town, anyway, and I doubt if anyone would bother pursuing me to her flat.'

Sari arrived late next day at her aunt's cottage near Newquay. Frank had taken her to Cheltenham and seen her off. It had been a rush, but Sari had been anxious to get away as soon as possible. She had packed overnight and they had left early before Anna was up. She had felt like a coward, not waiting to say goodbye, leaving Frank to explain her sudden departure, but he had assured her he would think of something. She had promised to keep in touch as she knew he was secretly worried about her. He was hurt that she was unable to confide in him, but how could she, Sari asked herself despairingly, tell him what had happened while he had been away? If she had been able to, he would probably have rushed to London and confronted Brent who, more than likely, would have laughed at him and sacked him immediately.

The journey was long and tiring and by the time she reached the cottage she was almost ready to collapse with exhaustion. Her whole body ached, her heart worst of all, making her feel she was on the verge of a terrible illness. The outside of the cottage looked cold and somehow unwelcoming, and she would have given anything for even a glimpse of Anna and Frank's kindly faces. It would be part of her punishment, she thought distractedly, to know Frank was working for the man who had ruined her. And Carnford would be a constant reminder, which was why she had not yet told Frank she could never return there.

Dumping her things against the cottage door, she went to get the keys from their nearest neighbour down the road. Mrs Barrie fortunately was in, and after saying hello, Sari briefly explained the purpose of her visit. 'Most of the furniture will have to be sold,' she said, 'unless someone takes it with the house.'

'Well, it's all good,' Mrs Barrie smiled, 'your aunt wouldn't have anything that wasn't, but with winter coming on it might take harm standing in empty property.'

'Yes, I know . . .' Sari agreed.

Mrs Barrie, a motherly woman, bustled about, filling a basket with a varied assortment of provisions. 'These'll tide you over till the morning, dear,' she said. When Sari protested, she laughed. 'I'm off to my sister's for a week, and milk and butter doesn't travel well. I'd have to give it to somebody. I'm leaving tomorrow,' she went on, as Sari thanked her, 'so it's lucky you caught me.'

'I'll pay you back when you return,' Sari said gratefully. 'I expect to be here a few weeks.'

In the cottage she closed the door and put a match to the fire, then sat and stared at it. Perversely she felt glad

Mrs Barrie was going away, as for the next few days she didn't think she would want to see anyone. The frozen anguish inside her was just beginning to melt. She could feel it tearing through her body and feared she was going to be helpless against the ravages of it. It would take time, she realised, to regain any kind of composure, and though she wouldn't see Brent again, the image of his face returned continually to haunt her.

For the next three days Sari lived in a complete vacuum. At first she tried to conquer the indescribable pain that swept over her by ignoring it, but when inevitably it grew too much for her, she lay sobbing on her bed, or simply staring blindly at the ceiling.

She didn't sleep well and wasn't eating. The basket Mrs Barrie had given her was still almost full, but she did get a pint of milk each day from the milkman. She drank this and ate biscuits, with no thought of what such a meagre diet was doing to her figure. As she had most of the money she had earned at Carnford still intact, she could easily afford to buy food, but she just wasn't hungry. Her appetite would return, she believed, as soon as she began feeling better.

It wasn't until the end of the week that she decided impatiently that it was high time she stopped being so sorry for herself, and that work might be a better antidote for her troubles than tears. The next morning it was Friday, and she rose early and began going through her aunt's clothing. Most of it would have to be burned, she thought ruefully. Aunt Joan had been extremely tall and thin, Sari knew no one who looked remotely like her. Apart from that, most of her aunt's things were so well worn she doubted if anyone would really want them. Even the long dresses which she had insisted on changing into for dinner were too shabby to be of any use to anyone.

The few items she considered worth salvaging, she put aside to offer to Mrs Barrie. Mrs Barrie had cleaned for her aunt in the days when they had been able to afford help, and she might like something. Sari wasn't sure what else, other than small things, she was free to give away. Aunt Joan had left the house to Frank, but she had taken out a second mortgage and her solicitors weren't sure how much there would be left. Sari hoped there would be enough to provide a small nest-egg for when he was married. Frank insisted she must accept half of the final sum, but she didn't want to. Lydia's family were very well-to-do and Sari felt it might help Frank's pride considerably if he was able to offer her a little more than just a manager's salary.

Sari worked hard during the following days and tried not to think of Brent. Being busy in the house helped, but in the evenings, when she forced herself to take a walk for some fresh air, he returned to her thoughts like a magnet. No matter how she tried to absorb herself totally in other things, he always seemed to be there, on the edge of her consciousness, like a menacing shadow that refused to go away.

It was just over a week after she had left Carnford that he arrived in the village. If she hadn't been looking out of the window at the time, he was driving so slowly she might never have heard his car. The house was on a narrow road, little more than a lane, and there was no other traffic. He must be hoping to surprise her, she realised, as he drew up almost noiselessly outside the gate and sat for a moment, motionless, staring towards the house.

Sari drew back, feeling stunned as if from a blow. He couldn't have seen her! She watched, her mouth falling open, in a way she had read of in books, as he opened the car door and swiftly unwound himself from behind the steering wheel.

Someone must have told him where she was. Sari kept on staring, unable to move. She was gripped by a terrible inertia that made it impossible for her even to think. The front door wasn't locked, but if he knocked and received no answer he might go away again. If he thought the house was empty, he might not come back. It didn't occur to her that it was almost as easy for Brent to see her as it was for her to see him. The windows were wide and the paleness of her dress betrayed her.

Her breath coming in short, painful gasps, she waited for him to knock. She had a frightening feeling that when he did she might faint. Yet, surprisingly, it was his heavy, demanding knock that brought her back to her senses. Immediately she heard it her mind and limbs began working again. Frantically, like a small, hunted animal, she stared about the room, looking for a place to hide. Finding none, she panicked, knowing she couldn't face him.

On stumbling feet she ran to the other door at the rear of the house. It stood open, allowing her headlong flight to the bottom of the garden. Here a path cut down through the cliff face to the shore. It was almost vertical, but provided a safe passage to the beach below if negotiated with reasonable care.

With Brent's harsh shout hurtling after her, Sari's descent, this evening, was neither reasonable or careful. As she caught a glimpse of his tall, pursuing figure over her shoulder, the need to escape him aroused in her a reckless madness she couldn't control. At the top of the cliff she simply took off and, not surprisingly, landed in a crumpled heap at the bottom. She didn't remember hitting the bottom as everything went black long before she got there.

When Sari became aware of the world again, she was only conscious of a delicious feeling of warmth. She felt she was floating on cottonwool clouds and had no idea where she was. Realisation came suddenly as she opened her eyes and discovered she was in bed, but, inadvertently, this increased her bewilderment as she was unable to recall how she had got there. She was sure she hadn't been in bed when ... Brent ...?

Something stirred beside her, interrupting the

apprehensive turn of her thoughts. In dawning horror her drowsy eyes lifted from the pristine whiteness of her bedspread to encounter him sleeping a yard away in a chair. Stunned, she gazed at him in startled amazement. What on earth was he doing here?

Then she remembered. He had come to the house and she hadn't answered when he'd knocked. He must have opened the front door and seen her disappearing through the back one. Vividly now she recalled being terrified by the sight of him pounding after her down the garden path. He had shouted a warning, but she had taken no notice. She hadn't stopped, and his harsh tones must have been responsible for her disastrous attempt to take a short cut to the shore. As the panic of that moment caught up with her again, she moved, and the pain that immediately shot through her seemed proof enough that the consequences of her crazy action might be even more serious than she suspected.

Clenching her dry lips to prevent a whimper of hurt escaping, she wondered dully why Brent hadn't gone back to London. Surely she had demonstrated clearly enough that she had no wish to see him. Why was he sitting by her bed, slumped in a chair, obviously asleep? Didn't he realise how much she hated him and never wanted to see him again?

Yet for a few minutes, as she stared at him, she was acutely conscious of nothing but his presence, the mystery of how she had got from the bottom of the cliff to her bed momentarily forgotten. Had any man the right to look so attractive? she thought bitterly. How much easier it might have been to hate him if he had been ugly. Helplessly, pressing back against her pillows, she continued to study his hard-hewn features and was forced to admit his face was compelling, even in sleep. Her throat muscles constricted when her eyes settled on his firm yet sensuous mouth and she remembered how it had felt when he had kissed her.

Such memories, crowding in on her, threatening to

rip her apart, jerked her upright with fright. Unfortunately her sudden movement increased the pain in her bruised limbs, and her anguished cry, which she wasn't able this time to smother, woke him.

In a daze she saw him sit up and sweep a confused hand over his forehead. In sleep his face had softened a little, but as she gazed at him the hard lines of his jaw, the aggressive jut of his chin became very marked again while his big body tensed warily. It seemed like a grim omen when his eyes hardened too, as he returned her blank stare.

CHAPTER SEVEN

'SARI?' He spoke at last, with a little of the same harshness in his voice which she had heard when he had called for her to stop as she had flown from him down the garden path.

'What are you doing here?' she asked, anger beginning to sweep through her. 'Why have you followed me?'

'I'll tell you in good time,' he countered. 'First I want to know, did you intend killing yourself when you jumped off that cliff?'

'No, I did not!' she retorted scornfully. 'You were chasing me and I didn't want to see you, Surely you're not so insensitive you can't realise that?'

She thought he flinched at the cold contempt in her voice, but couldn't be sure. Certainly he went white. 'I only wanted to talk to you,' he said grimly.

'Was that all?' she jeered, her face suddenly as pale as his. 'How could I be sure?'

'Perhaps I deserved that,' he conceded.

'Just perhaps!' Sari cried, her anger disguising pain.

'I'm sorry about what happened.' His voice was strangely uneven as he straightened in his chair then leant towards her, staring at her with darkening eyes. 'I'm not pretending it wasn't my fault, but I wish you'd been franker with me. You made a mystery of Santo and I jumped to the wrong conclusions.'

'I wasn't deliberately mysterious about anything,' she exclaimed. 'Santo imagines he loves me and would like to marry me, but I've never given him any encouragement. I'm not even very fond of him!'

'You didn't tell me that, though,' he held her flickering glance intently. 'There were occasions when I received quite the opposite impression.' When guilty colour swept her cheeks, he asked harshly, 'Would you like me to quote instances?'

'No!' With an effort Sari lowered her heavy lashes, plucking nervously at the sheets. 'If I gave the wrong impression, it was because you seemed to be accusing me of things of which I was innocent. You appeared to think badly of me, you implied I was a gold-digger.'

He sighed heavily. 'Yes, I did, and I went back to London, the day after our picnic, believing it was true. I'd believed it ever since I saw this.' From his pocket he dragged her mother's necklace and dropped it in her lap.

Sari's eyes widened as she gazed at it. 'You thought Santo had given it to me?'

'His grandmother left him some jewellery for his bride. I hadn't seen it for years, but I remembered a necklace, almost an exact replica of this.'

'And you thought I was flaunting it?'

'Yes,' his jaw muscles tightened grimly, 'it seemed sufficient proof to confirm my worst fears. I returned to London in a foul mood, determined to forget you. I was also determined that Santo should too. Then I found I couldn't stay away. I had to come back. You were in my blood, and for the first time in my life I couldn't get rid of the sight and sound of a woman.'

'How do you usually manage to?' she asked with a coldness which seemed to be coming quite naturally.

A faint redness crept under his skin, surprising her that she could embarrass him. 'For God's sake, Sari,' he rasped, 'will you listen!'

'Of course,' she taunted, her voice still gratifyingly cool. 'Do carry on.'

Anger flickered swiftly in his eyes but was as quickly gone. 'I returned to Carnford,' he said tersely, 'to see if we could make a fresh start, get to know each other better, if you like. I'll admit I used Frank as an excuse.

I did want to discuss something with him, but a phone call would have sufficed.'

'Was what you did,' she retorted sharply, 'all part of your plan?'

'I made no such plan,' he snapped. 'God, Sari, do you take me for a monster? Although,' he paused, his mouth twisting in self-derision, 'Maybe Santo's phone call turned me into one.'

'Santo's phone call?'

Brent nodded. 'On the Saturday afternoon, after I delivered that group of hikers to Joe. I heard you talking to Santo and I listened. I thought you were promising to marry him.'

'Marry him?' Sari's eyes went intensely green as she struggled to remember. 'He kept asking me to marry him and wouldn't take no for an answer. During the call you overheard, he threatened to come to Carnford. I didn't want him to, then I thought it might be a good idea, as that might be the only way I could convince him I didn't love him.'

Brent rose abruptly to pace the room. 'I was sure you intended marrying him for his money. You once said you knew how you could get some for Frank. I didn't think you loved Santo, not after the way you kissed me, which made what I believed you were going to do all the more despicable. For all our sakes I knew I had to do something, but I had no intention of going as far as I did.'

As his voice thickened and Sari choked convulsively, he returned to sit beside her, this time on the side of the bed. Curling a lean hand over her trembling ones, which still tensely clutched the sheets, he muttered hoarsely, 'Heaven help me, I didn't intend even going into your room, but I lost my head completely. As I carried you upstairs the last of my control vanished. I knew I had to have you, and I wasn't even thinking of Santo.'

'How can you say that,' she challenged icily, 'when

the first words you spoke afterwards concerned him?'

The hand covering hers tightened until she became aware of pain. 'I said what I did,' he rasped, 'because, in my crazy jealousy, it seemed to provide the ideal answer, for him as well as myself. And I had to find some excuse to justify what I'd done to you.'

In small, frozen tones, she asked, 'What did you hope for?'

He leant nearer to brush the thick hair from her hectically flushed cheeks while his eyes burned in his haggard face. 'I hoped to find myself cured of the passion I had for you. I was determined I wouldn't be a slave to any woman—or my emotions. I've seen how a craving for a certain woman can ruin a man by reducing him to an obedient puppet, and I'd always vowed it would never happen to me. It took me little more than twenty-four agonising hours to realise I was wrong about that, and a lot of other things. But when I returned to Carnford you'd gone.'

Sari was only half aware of the more revealing aspects of his confession as her anger and confusion grew. Blindly she tried to free herself from his hurting hands, but as her frantic movement caused pain to spear through her hurt limbs, to her dismay she fell completely against him.

Brent must have got the impression that she had flung herself into his arms as they swiftly enclosed her and tightened. 'I have to be careful,' he said huskily. 'My poor darling,' he groaned, 'you may not have broken any bones, but you've got a hell of a lot of bruises. All the same, I must kiss you.'

Before she could so much as stir, to her horror, his mouth crushed hers, cutting off her indignant protests. Too surprised to resist immediately, she began experiencing the same disturbing sensations she had felt before. As his lips pressed over hers, she felt the warmth and strength of him flowing into her and her body and mind began floating on a shimmering, intoxicating

cloud. It took every bit of resolution she possessed to
hold herself taut as he tried to mould her to him—to
tighten her trembling lips when he would have
passionately parted them. She had to remind herself
forcibly of what he had done to her before the coldness
which had briefly deserted her returned to enable her to
push him away.

As his arms dropped to his sides, he stared at her
white face while his own flushed a dull red. 'You hate
me, don't you?'

Fiercely she nodded. 'You killed everything else
along with my self-respect. I think all men are hateful,'
she continued angrily. 'Even Frank isn't to be trusted.
He promised faithfully he wouldn't tell anyone where I
was!'

The disturbed pitch in Brent's voice was swiftly
checked. 'You mustn't blame your brother, Sari. He
didn't tell me until your cousin did.'

'Cilla?'

'That's her name,' his mouth thinned. 'I more or less
haunted her flat, after Frank led me to believe you were
there. When eventually your cousin turned up, from
some modelling assignment abroad, I was surprised to
learn that you'd never actually lived in London. In fact
you'd only stayed with her a week.'

'My visit wasn't a success,' Sari hedged unhappily.
'Cilla's only my second cousin and we haven't a great
deal in common.'

'Nothing, I should say,' Brent muttered curtly.

Cilla was beautiful. It hurt to know he could find no
comparison. And he must have noticed, because Cilla's
looks were the kind that dazzled. 'She told you I—I'd
lived in Cornwall?'

'After a lot of persuasion—expensive persuasion.'

'And Frank filled in the rest?'

'More or less. He believed you were trying to avoid
Santo. I had my work cut out convincing him it was
really me you were running from, but that we were

going to be married.'

She flushed. 'I thought it was best . . .'

'Another of your harmless little deceptions, Sari?' he observed unpleasantly. 'Didn't you ever wonder where all these clever little half-truths might lead to?'

'That's not fair!' she replied agitatedly. 'I hated deceiving Frank, but how could I have told him the truth? And I didn't actually lie about Santo. I had no particular desire to see him and I had always intended coming back here to sort out my aunt's things.'

'I see,' said Brent expressionlessly.

'You haven't told Santo anything?' she asked suddenly, her face paling.

'I've told him all he needs to know,' he snapped enigmatically. 'Not what I'd done to you, of course. I'm no keener than anyone else to parade my own sins.'

Sari supposed she should be relieved. It bothered her vaguely that she should feel nothing. She didn't even flinch from Brent's grimly ironical tones. All she wanted was to be left alone, to submerge herself in isolation and loneliness again. At least that didn't hurt.

She stared at him, beginning to feel very weary and ill, her melancholy face reflecting her feelings, an open book for him to read. 'So you came all the way to Cornwall to apologise and return my necklace, which I presume Santo managed to convince you wasn't the one his grandmother had left to him?'

'I didn't mention the necklace either,' Brent hesitated. 'I checked, and my mother's is still there along with the rest of the stuff. I'd broken the clasp of yours and had it fixed for you. The jeweller, one of the best in London, and whom I know well, assures me that the stones in yours aren't,' he reddened curiously, 'worth very much.'

Sari shrugged. 'I've never given much thought to its value, and I can't thank you for having it mended as you broke it deliberately in the first place.'

'My God, Sari!' Brent's face was so grim he looked ten years older than his actual years. 'You certainly know how to make a man squirm!'

'You wouldn't,' she retorted coldly, 'if you weren't ashamed of yourself.' As his grey eyes blazed and then went sombre, she could no longer find the strength to go on taunting him. Weakly she sighed. 'Now that you've presumably said all you came to say, would you mind going? I'm feeling tired and would like to rest.'

'Going?' again a grim kind of anger tightened his mouth. 'Where the hell do you think I'd be going to?'

Sari blinked with startled reaction. All the time he had been at Carnford she could never remember hearing him curse. In the past hour he seemed to have done little else. 'Back to London, of course.'

'Only when you're well enough to come with me.'

'Don't be silly,' she thought he was offering a lift, 'I can't go anywhere until this house is sold.'

'We can arrange it together. Once you're well enough I'll help you tidy up, and a good estate agent will take care of the rest.'

This was enough to make Sari try to jump out of bed, a mistake which, as before, tore from her a cry of pain and alarm and prompted Brent to swift action.

Pushing her back against her pillows, he threatened to hold her there with both hands if she dared move again. 'Last night you nearly killed yourself,' he ground out, his grey eyes smouldering on her blanching face. 'Your doctor doesn't know how you didn't. You have severe bruising and shock and he warned me you must stay in bed, at least for a day or two.'

'Have you been here all night?' she whispered, too pain-racked to go on fighting him.

'Naturally,' he replied shortly. 'And it's now two o'clock the next day.'

'Who—who put me to bed?' she faltered, a faint colour creeping to her pale cheeks.

'I laid you on your bed,' Brent answered dryly, 'but don't worry, I wasn't the one who undressed you. The nurse who came with the doctor did that. I wasn't fool enough to try when you might have had severe injuries. The nurse should be back to see you soon, but the doctor doesn't think you need more than rest and someone to look after you. When I assured him I would do that, as I happened to be your fiancé, he was quite satisfied.'

The next time Sari woke the bitterness of their ensuing quarrel returned immediately. She had said at once that she had never heard of anything so ridiculous and would tell Doctor Adams the truth!

'Go right ahead,' Brent had taunted icily, 'but it won't make any difference, I'm still staying.'

'I wouldn't marry you,' she had gasped unoriginally, 'if you were the last man on earth!'

'An engagement isn't marriage,' he had replied coldly, with a wary eye on her increasing agitation. 'Ours can easily be broken, but meanwhile, it does lend an air of respectability to the situation. Something,' he observed grimly, 'which I believe means a lot to you.'

'Oh, why don't you just go!' Sari had moaned impatiently.

'Because there's no one else to look after you,' he had replied tersely, 'and we haven't even begun talking yet.'

With a sigh he had risen from the bed and left her, returning after a few minutes with a warm drink. She had wanted to go on arguing with him, but had suddenly been too weak to do anything other than obediently swallow the milky liquid, when he put an arm around her and held the cup to her lips.

He had left her only when the district nurse had arrived to make her comfortable.

'I see your fiancé is taking good care of you,' the nurse smiled, adding in a stage-whisper as Brent went from the room, 'If he were my fiancé, dear, it would do me good just to look at him. What a blessing he arrived when he did, otherwise you might have lain at the foot of the cliff for hours before anyone found you. I always said that path wasn't safe!'

If only Nurse Jones knew! She mightn't feel so kindly disposed towards Brent, Sari thought angrily, if she realised he was merely pretending to be her fiancé—for reasons known only to himself, which he hadn't disclosed.

When Nurse Jones had been ready to go, he had seen her out, and Sari had fallen asleep listening to the low murmur of their voices downstairs in the hall. Reaching for a drink, from the jug of cool water Brent had placed by her bedside, she wondered apprehensively where he was now. She felt like a coward for not denouncing him to Nurse Jones, but the moment when the opportunity was there had passed. Fear of the publicity such a dramatic confession might attract had kept her reluctantly silent. But as soon as she was a little better, she was determined to leave if he wouldn't!

Two days passed before Sari was able to leave her bed and get about fairly normally again. The bruises on her legs were fading gradually, the pain from them reduced to a bearable ache, but she still felt strangely lethargic. While she had been in bed, although Brent had rarely left her side for more than a few minutes at a time, he had been entirely uncommunicative. She had been reassured when he had promised that as soon as she was well again their engagement would end, but she found his silence made her so uneasy it almost cancelled her feelings of relief.

She couldn't think why she was so uneasy, because he didn't make another attempt to kiss—or even touch her. Perhaps it was her own vulnerableness that worried her most, though she couldn't really explain that either.

On the third morning she thought she detected a great improvement and decided she would try and complete the few small jobs left to do. By tomorrow, if she continued to improve, she might be strong enough to get away. But all the next day, as if he guessed her intentions, Brent watched her like a hawk. Long before evening arrived, Sari felt near screaming point from being under such constant observation.

After dinner, which he insisted on cooking, he asked casually, 'Well, have you decided to make a break for it?'

'No, I haven't!' she snapped contrarily. 'Why should I? I don't intend spending the rest of my life running away from you!'

'I'm glad to hear it,' he replied quietly.

He sounded so reasonable that she screwed up sufficient courage to suggest, 'I can manage by myself now. You don't have to stay any longer.'

Ignoring this, Brent made her leave the dinner table and sit in a comfortable chair by the fire. 'I think the time has come for that talk I mentioned,' he said, his grey eyes glittering down into her wide green ones.

He stood over her and she tried not to look at his tall, vital figure. He might have a handsome appearance, but, she reminded herself scornfully, he was nothing but a brute and a bully! He had used his charm ruthlessly to get his own way and she felt for him nothing but contempt. She hated to think he had ever touched her. To remember that she had let him make love to her made her shiver!

He sat down opposite her while she tried desperately to fan her hate and contempt into a blaze. When the heat from the fire seemed to stifle him into loosening his tie and the top buttons of his shirt, she cried sharply, 'You don't have to undress to impress me. You'd be wasting your time!'

'Sari—please!'

Heedlessly she rushed on, her eyes green ice, 'Will you just say whatever it is you still have left to say, and go? Then I can get on with my life and forget we ever met. It's going to be hard enough as it is.'

Brent replied with a gentleness which contrasted oddly with her bitterness, 'Don't you see, Sari, I can't go. The engagement you believe I contrived has to be permanent. We have to be married.'

'Married?' horrified, she exclaimed in a breathless whisper. 'You must be mad!'

A familiar hardness formed along his jaw and his eyes darkened formidably at her obvious derision. 'We were both mad, that night at Carnford. Now it's up to us to put things right. We're to be married in a week's time. I have everything arranged.'

'You can't be serious!' she gasped through dry lips.

'I've never been more serious in my life,' he retorted with a grim soberness. 'I've never asked a woman to marry me before.'

'You're not asking—you're telling!' Sari's face was colourless and disturbed. 'I hadn't forgotten about Carnford,' she flung at him. 'do you think I ever could, but I'm sure you don't propose to every woman you take advantage of!'

He said harshly. 'The few women I've had affairs with have known exactly what they were doing.'

'Which still doesn't explain why you feel you must marry me!'

'It should,' he rejoined bluntly. 'Even you must realise there could be consequences from our care-lessness.'

'You must be crazy!' but shock rushed through Sari as she stared at him.

'Well, that makes a change from madness,' he noted curtly, 'but I'm taking no chances.'

Sari felt as weak as she had done when she had first left her bed. Her head was pounding, her hands clammy. 'We don't love each other!'

'Speak for yourself,' Brent retorted gravely. 'I love you.'

This seemed such a mockery after what had taken place that she laughed wildly. 'Don't ever tell me that again. It's an insult and I hate you! We could never be in love and get married.'

His face went so white and hard, she had a moment's terrible misgiving, but she ignored the pain in his eyes and emphasised for good measure, 'Never!'

'I'm sorry, Sari,' he said stiffly, 'I'm afraid you have no choice in the matter. I refuse to risk having any son of mine born out of wedlock.'

'But I'm not having your son!' she choked, her face suddenly scarlet.

'You can't be sure.'

The worry of waiting and wondering was already eating into her very soul, but she couldn't tell him that. Stubbornly she shook her head, unaware that the wide apprehension in her eyes betrayed her.

He watched her grimly for a few moments before suggesting, 'Supposing we consider this from other angles?'

'What other angles?' She jumped to her feet suspiciously. 'I don't want to talk about it any more.'

'It might pay you to sit down again and listen,' he retorted. When, feeling trapped and somehow helpless, she obeyed, he continued ruthlessly, 'If you don't marry me could you face the world if you discovered you were pregnant? And don't say you'd have an abortion, because you aren't the type.' As she stared at him dully, unable to argue, his eyes narrowed. 'Let's believe you aren't pregnant, Sari, and you meet someone else. Could you marry another man with telling him he wasn't the first?'

Sari clenched her hands in agony, as if the decision already faced her. 'Men don't mind, nowadays.'

'Some still do,' he disagreed, 'but if you'd been married and divorced this problem wouldn't arise. A lot of men,' he observed cynically, 'seem able to forgive several husbands, but not a girl who's single and confesses to having slept around.'

'Once could scarcely be construed as sleeping around!' she muttered painfully.

'You'd have no proof.'

He obviously had no intention of sparing her! 'You—you mentioned divorce?' she whispered.

'You can have one after a year,' he said harshly, 'along with an income for life.'

'And you believe that will persuade me?'

'I think it might.'

Bitterly she pushed back her wealth of red-gold curls. 'You think money can buy anything! Haven't you a conscience?'

Brent merely ignored this impassively. 'If money won't persuade you there are other ways. This house, I believe, belonged to your aunt and now belongs to your brother?'

Sari bit her lip nervously. It might be futile to deny it, as Frank must have told him. 'Yes.'

'Why,' Brent asked disapprovingly, 'when you lived with her, didn't she leave it to you? Your doctor said you'd even nursed her through her last long illness.'

'Because——' Sari hesitated, confused by a sense of loyalty and such rapid questions, 'I—she thought my mother's necklace was valuable enough to provide for me. And she used to say girls got married and didn't need as much money as men.'

Brent's mouth twisted contemptuously, but she was relieved that he didn't openly criticise her aunt, who might not have been very practical but had always had the best of intentions.

She thought Brent had lost interest in the subject and she was bewildered when, after a short silence, he returned to it.

'How does Frank feel about this?'

She had an urge to tell Brent it was none of his business, but instead found herself answering defensively. 'He wants me to take half. He really does!' she insisted as Brent's dark brows rose sceptically. 'I'm trying to refuse, but he won't listen.'

Brent said slowly, his eyes never leaving her distressed face, 'If you had a wealthy husband, Sari, and Frank knew you didn't need the money, do you think that might persuade him to take all of it?'

So that was what all his interest in the house had been leading up to? Was it any wonder Brent was wealthy if he applied the same deviousness in business! Coldly her eyes met his. 'Frank would be the last to approve if I allowed myself to be bribed for his sake.'

'Not even if the whole sum of money would allow him to take over Carnford?'

'Take—over—Carnford?'

'You don't have to sound so surprised,' Brent said suavely. 'I've been thinking of offering him the tenancy or a partnership, even something on a share basis, but naturally I've had to consider his pride.'

'His—pride?'

'I realised he would require money and, apart from his salary, he doesn't appear to have any. To take over any kind of business a man needs some capital of his own. Even if the banks let him borrow, I doubt if they'd be willing to lend him enough. The proceeds from the sale of this house, even after the mortgage still owing is repaid, should be sufficient to start him off nicely.'

If Sari had felt trapped before, she knew now there was no hope of escape. It would be possible to challenge Brent regarding his initial opinion of Frank, which had never suggested he would ever consider him as a tenant for Carnford, but she feared she would be wasting her time. He had simply been using Frank to disguise the real purpose behind his visit, which had been to put a stop to any further friendship between herself and Santo.

That his plan had misfired because he had briefly lost his head must have proved very galling. but he was a proud man and, she realised bitterly, she had never stood any real chance against him. He was determined to marry her so there could be no possible slight against his name. Other men might have been willing to wait until they were sure there was going to be a child, but, as he said, he didn't intend taking any chances! As for Frank—well, he couldn't own a mere farm manager as a brother-in-law, could he? Even the small elevation to farm tenant would be better than that!

There was an acid taste in her mouth as she said tensely, 'I have to marry you, don't I?'

Brent nodded coolly. 'If you'd agreed in the first place we might have avoided all this.'

She lifted her chin, her eyes wide with animosity. 'You must have had it all worked out!'

He paled as he met her condemning glance. 'You must see that nothing could be worse than days of haggling.'

The expression he used seemed an insult, especially when he had talked of loving her! Sari glared at him. Perhaps it was time she began quoting a few terms of her own.

'If you force me to marry you,' she said coldly, 'I won't live with you as your wife.'

Brent stared at her, inscrutably studying the small, tormented face which struggled to defy him. 'Why not leave such a decision until later? You've been through a lot.'

'It's not that.' Unexpected tears glistened in her eyes as she swallowed painfully. 'Don't you understand?' her voice rose on the edge of control. 'I—I can't bear to even think of letting you touch me!'

Suddenly she began sobbing wildly, and thinking bitterly that fate was dealing her yet another blow, she covered her face with her hands, helplessly.

With a smothered exclamation Brent lifted her, holding her against him. With his arms tightly around her he rubbed his cheek gently on her hot brow. 'Don't!' he pleaded huskily, as her slender body shook. 'It tears me in two to see you so unhappy. I'll try and make up for everything you've suffered, if only you'll give me a chance.'

She tried to speak, but couldn't find the breath, for she was fighting herself more than him. She had just declared she couldn't bear him to touch her, yet her clinging body seemed bent on betraying her. Was it possible, physically, to be oblivious of shame? When she was in Brent's arms a sweet, pulsating hunger flooded over her, making her senses clamour to surrender to the hold he appeared to have over them.

His voice reached her even as she struggled to prevent her hands from creeping around his neck. 'I won't bother you, Sari, I promise. I know I'm touching you now, but I'm not trying to make love to you. Would it help if I suggested that, for the present, you looked to me for comfort rather than love?'

'You mean,' her small, hiccuping voice asked, 'as a friend?'

'If you like.'

That tempted her to raise her head, but immediately her eyes fell on his hard, cruel mouth, the fierce desire which shot through her prompted her to protest. 'No, it's not possible!'

'For God's sake!' he muttered. 'You have to learn to trust me again. Life's not long enough, Sari, to waste time regretting what's past. You have to try and concentrate on the future.'

Because the bleakness of the future was beginning to haunt her, she shrank from him, a movement which goaded him to taunt, 'I don't believe what happened at Carnford could have killed everything you felt for me.'

She froze, her lips parting in stunned amazement. 'Can't you understand—the shame and disgrace!'

'There won't be any disgrace, either now or later,' snapped Brent his patience wearing thin as she refused to listen. 'Who the hell's supposed to know what happened between you and me? And if you're so worried about the disgrace, why in heaven's name did it take you so long to agree to marry me?'

'I don't know,' Sari admitted hollowly, speaking the truth. It was the only way, she saw now, but it didn't make her feel any better. That was the trouble, she realised dully. Married or unmarried, she doubted if she

would ever feel happy again. Brent derided her for
dwelling on the past. How could she tell him that she
tried not to think of it for a moment but that the future
seemed even less inviting? Perhaps, she gazed at him
lightheadedly, she had what was known as depression.

'I think I'll go to bed,' she said at last, 'if you don't
mind.'

'A good idea,' Brent agreed, releasing her, his face
expressionless. Only the glittering darkness of his eyes
indicated he was full of suppressed violence.

It took Sari almost all the next day to collect together
most of her aunt's personal belongings and dispose of
them in a way she hoped Aunt Joan would have
approved of. She was frustrated to find she still tired
easily, but by the time she had finished she was
comparatively satisfied with the amount of work she
had got through.

Brent cooked their meals and helped where he could,
but when he left that afternoon to see the estate agent in
Newquay, she was relieved. Since the night before he
had kept his distance, but she was frequently aware of
his grey eyes burning over her, and of something
incalculable in his manner which kept her nervously on
edge.

She would like to have believed she was the one in
charge of operations, but had to admit it was really the
other way round. Reluctantly she realised that both
their roles came naturally to them. She had been used
to her aunt dictating practically every breath she took,
while Brent had been head of a huge business empire
for so long that he could never be ordinarily
subservient. Once she found herself wondering what his
staff would think if they could see him now, dressed in
a pair of old slacks teamed with a V-necked sweater.
The sweater bothered her a little as he obviously wore
nothing underneath, and the neckline filled with crisp,
dark hairs emphasised his virile masculinity to a
disturbing degree. She wished he didn't have this effect

on her, as she vowed she would never allow any man to stir her again as he had done at Carnford.

He hadn't returned, but was waiting for her when she came up the cliff path from a walk along the shore.

'Are you always so foolhardy?' he asked, his face pale under his tan. 'You might have fallen again.'

The house had suddenly stiffled her—or her thoughts, she wasn't sure which, but she didn't confess that. 'You weren't chasing me this time,' she retorted sharply, the unconscious resentment which weighed so heavily on her soul, as always seeking an outlet. 'And aren't you forever hinting that the best way to come to terms with a situation is to face it?'

'I didn't expect you to take my advice so indiscriminately,' he bit out savagely. 'The next time you have an accident you might not be so lucky!'

'I suppose it's your improbable son and heir you're really worried about?' she breathed in reckless defiance.

CHAPTER EIGHT

SARI was astonished by the look of fury on Brent's face. She couldn't remember ever seeing him so angry and marvelled at the control he exercised. His mouth was cruel, his jaw tight, his eyes narrowed to thin slits through which he watched her like a lion about to devour it's prey.

She pushed a trembling hand through her red-gold curls. She was frightened, but knew she must conceal that from him at all cost. 'Wouldn't it be easier if you murdered me straight away,' she taunted blindly, 'rather than let me die by inches?'

'So that's how you think it will be, being married to me?' he said bitingly,

'Are you surprised?' She tried to keep the defiance in her voice and flung up her head nervously. 'Our divorce is like the light at the end of a tunnel. Otherwise . . .' she shrugged insolently.

'Okay,' he snapped roughly, his grey eyes smoking ice, 'if that's the way you see it, there's no reason why I should try and spare you. Tomorrow we return to Carnford, where you'll stay until it's time to come to London for our wedding.'

'Carnford?' She shrank from him, until his hand grabbed her wrist, jerking her back. Her face was white, all her false courage gone. 'I—you can't leave me there, Brent. I'd rather go straight to London. I could stay with Cilla. I could never face Frank and Anna!'

'You silly little fool!' his breath blasted her cold face like a furnace. 'You can't run for ever. There's nothing to get hysterical about. Do you think we're the first couple who've ever anticipated marriage? You don't have to indulge in dramatic confessions, so you can stop worrying about having to bare your straitlaced little soul. You don't have to tell them anything. They already know we're going to be married and that I'm taking you back there.'

'You were so sure of me?' Her face, flushed from his brutal attack, paled.

His mouth curved cynically. 'After what happened, I imagined I could be.'

Putting her free hand over her burning eyes, she moaned, 'Oh, how could you . . .?'

'Sari,' his anger falling away, his face went as white as her own, 'I had to act fast. Can't you understand that and at least try and meet me halfway? You may think you're suffering, but you don't know what I'm going through!'

'I'm sorry.' Her voice was stilted, but it was the best she could do. She supposed she was being selfish, but if it was true he was suffering, she couldn't help feeling sourly pleased. At thirty-six, if he had occasionally thought of marriage it wouldn't have been with a girl like herself. She was glad she wasn't the only one who was feeling trapped!

As if he was determined to follow his own advice, Brent's eyes softened on hearing her apology and ran over her possessively. Taking her hand from her face, he pressed it over his sweater above his heart, which she could feel beating heavily. Slowly he pushed it up until her palms encountered the softly curling cloud of hair at his throat. Then he thrust it inside the V and waited for her fingers to dig convulsively into his warm skin and her face to flush from the unexpected assault on her too vulnerable senses.

With her hands trapped, one by the wrist, the other under his sweater, she was helpless as he lowered his head and cut off her breath and protest with the hardness of his mouth. Sari began experiencing familiar disturbing sensations, the heat and weakness she was determined to despise. His hands were like steel holding her against him while his lips crushed hers in a kiss which was both devastating and irresistibly enticing.

Pressed hard against him, lips joined, she could feel his warmth seeping into her, demanding and receiving her response. She felt the authority in the arms that held her, and wondered dizzily if he meant her to. She was aware of the knowledge in the mouth which laid such indisputable claim to hers, and body and mind surrendered to both. She tried to fight, to reinforce the frail barricade she was so determinedly building against him and failed miserably. He took her mouth, dealing with it relentlessly, as her slight struggles again appeared to arouse his anger, and, unable to combat such turbulence, she felt it whirl her like a cyclone towards the sun, spinning her until she was consumed by fire.

Brent was breathing deeply when he suddenly let her go, and her eyes were panic-stricken as she realised the hold he still had over her.

'You—you promised you wouldn't touch me!' she reminded him wildly.

'I'm doing my best,' he said with a savage smile, as her eyes lifted to his face in bitter accusation, 'but you don't make it easy for me. When I came home and couldn't find you, I thought you might have drowned. The tide's running high, and you don't seem to care. You make me say and do things I regret.'

'You regret me completely, don't you?' she flared acridly.

She heard him draw a long sharp breath, but he didn't move. 'You're doing your best to make me,' he said steadily, 'but I'd never wish you any harm.'

Her nerves suddenly snapped. 'Don't worry,' she flung at him, using the only weapon she thought she had, 'I doubt if you're worth the sacrifice of my life, and I certainly wouldn't take any chances with another's!'

For a moment she thought he was going to hit her,

but he eventually managed to control his rising temper and with a smothered groan grabbed her again, but this time only to guide her up the garden path.

'I found a Chinese restaurant in Newquay and thought I'd treat myself to a night off. I brought a few things for our supper, although you may have to eat it yourself. You've taken away my appetite.'

So there must be ways of cracking his usually impregnable shell, Sari thought with bitter surprise. Perhaps if she had patience she might find other ways of making him suffer as much as she was doing.

They drove to Carnford next day. Sari said a silent goodbye to the house where she had lived for so many years. The house agent assured them it would soon sell as it was large and comfortable and stood in its own grounds, but Sari couldn't honestly say that the idea of someone else living there was abhorrent to her. There had never been enough warmth, in either the house or her aunt, to make her regret leaving. The charm of the vast sands and the brilliant colouring of the sea was another matter. Already, at Carnford, she had missed the magnificence of the wind which when it blew hard from the north or west, swept the Atlantic into line after line of awe-inspiring breakers which hurled dramatically against the high, wild cliffs. During storms she had often spent hours at her bedroom window watching the turbulent waves, but most of all, at such times, she had loved being in the garden, feeling the spray-tossed challenge of it in her hair and face.

As they passed over Bodmin Moor, Brent said, 'When we reach Carnford I won't stay.'

'Won't Frank think it funny if you rush straight off?' Sari asked uncertainly.

'Why should he?' he countered. 'I think you'll find, after I offer him the tenancy of the place, he'll be so excited he won't spare us much thought. If you're clever enough to pretend you're in love with me, you shouldn't have any problems.'

'Do you think you're being very clever, leaving me there on my own?' she retorted, feeling outraged that he should even suggest she should pretend to be in love with him, 'How can you be sure I won't change my mind about marrying you and run away?'

'If you do,' his voice didn't change, but his hands went white on the steering wheel, 'I'd find you and chain you to my side—and Frank wouldn't get a thing but his notice.'

'He could always find another job.'

'He could.'

Why didn't Brent just laugh at her and be done with it? Sari wondered hollowly. Jobs weren't exactly two a penny, and for a man like Frank, about to be married, the loss of his job could ruin his whole future. He wasn't the kind of man who would be content to run the house while his wife earned enough to keep them.

'I won't run away,' she promised dully.

Very soon, Brent pulled off the road for lunch. The hotel he chose was large and not too busy. 'It looks all right,' he shrugged indifferently. 'We'll just have to chance our luck.'

Sari didn't mind stopping, as she had no desire to reach Carnford any sooner than was necessary. She still feared guilt might be written all over her face and that she would see nothing but disapproval and condemnation on Frank and Anna's.

'Couldn't I have stayed with you in London?' she tried again to appeal to Brent.

'No,' he said shortly, crumbling a piece of bread rather savagely between his fingers. 'The day before the wedding will be soon enough. My staff would take one look at you and guess you had no wish to marry me.'

If only things had been different! But hadn't he killed all the love which made a girl's face glow? 'I've never been very good at hiding my feelings,' she said coldly, tasting her soup then laying down her spoon.

'Exactly,' he replied bleakly, his glance frowning on

her bent head, 'but you must try and practise how to at
Carnford. You'll have almost three days, long enough
to come to terms with the inevitable and to learn how
to smile again.'

'You think so?' She stared at the tablecloth, rather
than look at him. She only allowed her eyes to go as far
as his hands. Long, lean fingers with well kept nails and
a wrist encircled by the leather strap of a watch she
wouldn't have liked to put a price to. Remembering the
steely strength of those hands, she hastily averted her
fixed gaze, wishing she had done so in the first place.
There didn't seem a part of him which a part of her
didn't react to. It filled her with a sense of foreboding
for the future.

Frank was coming from the house as they arrived
and for a moment Sari went white and shrank, with
mixed feelings, from the delight she saw on his homely
features as he hurried forward to meet them. With
Brent's punishing grip on her arm and his tersely
whispered, 'Behave yourself!' in her ear, she quickly
tried to pull herself together. She would never give him
the satisfaction of a scene, she thought bitterly. With an
effort she forced a smile as Frank hugged her happily.

Anna was waiting decorously in the hall. Sari almost
burst into tears on noticing she was wearing her best
black with a snowy white apron. She had even greater
difficulty in holding back tears when Anna, in her
slightly old-fashioned way, wished them every happiness. Anna was obviously impressed and didn't appear
at all suspicious regarding the suddenness of Sari's
engagement. Sari, however, was glad when she scuttled
back to her kitchen. Anna, she suspected, would be
harder to fool than Frank, but perhaps for two days she
could manage it.

Brent declined her offer of tea. After a word with
Frank, he said, he would like to get straight on.
Requesting her firmly to stay where she was, he asked
Frank if they could go to the office. Sari poked around

the drawing-room until they came out.

Frank, not unexpectedly, appeared slightly dazed. He still did a few minutes later, as Sari went outside with Brent to see him off.

'Frank's going to bring you to London on Thursday for our wedding on Friday,' Brent paused beside the car. 'I'll see you then.'

Sari tried to school her features to hide an increasing resentment and despair as he dropped a cool kiss on her cheek. 'May I ask Lydia?' she asked.

'I've already left her an invitation with Frank,' he said, 'but you can always mention it yourself.'

He didn't really care. His eyes were as expressionless as his voice. Sari stared at him, then her lashes swept her pale cheeks. Inside he must be even more consumed by resentment than she was. How deeply he must be regretting allowing a need to protect his nephew and a brief moment of overwhelming desire to shatter the caution of a lifetime—of half a lifetime. Her lips curved ironically as she remembered that man's years were supposed to be three score and ten.

Noticing her faint smile, Brent gazed at her intently. A subtle change came over him while a muscle jerked at the side of his tightly held mouth. 'Sari,' he muttered suddenly, hoarsely, 'there's nothing at the office that can't be cancelled, if you'd like me to stay.'

'Stay?' she flinched as fright overtook her and two days of freedom became more precious than anything else. 'No!' she cried, and enjoyed seeing his face grow grim, while her eyes sparkled with dislike.

For the rest of the day she tried to bolster up the feeling of triumph that had shot through her as wordlessly Brent had dropped into his powerful car and drove off. His pride should suffer a lot more before their marriage was over, she vowed. She couldn't really understand why the thought of a divorce should increase her mounting pain, when it should have had quite the opposite effect.

Frank was so incredibly delighted with Brent's offer of a tenancy that he was unable to concentrate on Sari's affairs for very long. She wondered if this was what Brent had intended. Certainly Frank's mind appeared to be running exactly along the lines Brent had forecast.

'You could have knocked me down with a feather', he grinned, 'when Brent told me you were going to be married but had quarrelled and you were really running from him. Mind you,' he frowned, 'I still didn't tell him where you were as you'd asked me not to and I could see something was wrong. But when Cilla spilled the beans, I had to confirm it. After all, he is my boss!'

Sari felt trapped to an even greater degree as he rushed happily on. 'Maybe I shouldn't say this, love, but it's great news that you won't be needing any money from Aunt Joan's house. I should just be able to take over Carnford with what's left after everything's settled.'

Well, it was no use pretending Brent had blackmailed her into marriage through Frank. Offering Carnford to Frank had merely been adding a touch of respectability. It might have been an added incentive, but Brent's main concern was his possible son and heir!

'I'm glad you're pleased, Frank.' She managed a smile and hoped he didn't notice it was strained.

'You'd better remember to thank Cilla when you see her,' Frank continued in an expansive mood, 'although I don't think she went unpaid for her trouble. She rang after she eventually told him you might be in Cornwall—curiosity, I suppose. She seems quite dazzled by him. I should watch her, if I were you.'

In a way, Lydia was no more tactful when she arrived. 'I can just make the wedding,' she laughed. 'I mean, I don't want to jeopardise the week I'm trying to cajole for ours, do I, darling?' she twinkled at Frank.

Sari wondered how they would manage. Lydia was ambitious and worked long, odd hours, while Frank was steeped in routine to a degree. That he had broken it this summer to meet the demands of Lydia's career might be a good sign, but Sari wondered if he would be so willing to adapt himself after he was married. This was none of her business, of course, but she couldn't help feeling worried.

'You'll have to make sure you do get a week off,' she heard Frank saying heatedly.

'If not we'll have to make do with a weekend,' Lydia replied blithely.

'What about when you have a family?' Sari exclaimed, then flushed a deep red as this reminded her painfully of her own situation. Lydia would never be such a naïve fool as she had been—there was no comparison. She wished fervently that she had kept quiet as she saw the other two looking at her curiously.

It was Lydia who broke the rather fraught silence. 'We aren't in any hurry to start a family,' she said lightly, 'especially now Frank's going to take over the estate. I should warn you, though,' she quirked at Sari, 'all men aren't the same. I can't see your Mr Holding being prepared to wait.'

Frank hurriedly excused himself as the telephone rang, nearly tripping over in his haste to leave the room.

Lydia said, in surprised tones, 'What's the matter with him?'

Sari glanced at the door Frank had closed perhaps a shade too sharply. 'Well, I am his sister and he probably feels a bit embarrassed. He often seems to act as if I were only sixteen.'

'Not now, surely?' Lydia's brows rose disbelievingly, 'Phew! I quite envy you in a way. Well ...' as Sari frowned, 'who wouldn't? Brent Holding, he's quite a catch, I can tell you, and I work for the media, so I should know!' At Sari's puzzled expression, she shook her head impatiently. 'You're such an unworldly little thing, Sari, I wonder if you realise. All that money, to say nothing of looks and sex appeal and oodles of charm. If you want my opinion . . .'

Sari didn't, but had no wish to be rude to Lydia, whom she really liked. 'Brent's a business man, first and foremost,' she explained without pausing to think how, what she was saying would sound. 'You don't have to make him out to be anything else.'

'Darling,' said Lydia, 'if you really think that you have a shock coming! I'm older than you, Sari,' she continued as Sari frowned. 'You've probably gaps which would normally have been filled in by your mother so perhaps I ought to warn you not to be too surprised if you find you've gone slightly astray in your estimations regarding your future husband. These super controlled men are often the worst when their control goes.'

On Thursday they left Carnford for London. Lydia was surprised that Sari wasn't buying her wedding dress in London, but Brent had told her there wouldn't be time and she would be better to find something in Cheltenham. He had wanted to give her some money, but she had refused.

'I won't be able to afford the kind of clothes you'll probably expect your wife to wear,' she had retorted proudly, 'but at least I've enough for my wedding dress, even if it can't be white.'

She recalled the harsh lines of his face as she had said that and felt a tremor of sharp satisfaction. Already she had discovered how he hated being reminded of what he had done to her. It was going to be a very useful weapon for the future.

'Choose whatever you like,' he had agreed, his mouth taut with what, for a mistaken moment, she had imagined was pain.

Sari had chosen what she liked but had limited her purchases to quality rather than quantity. Her one impulsive buy had been a satin and lace nightdress which she had suddenly decided she would taunt him with. Now she wished she hadn't. For one thing, she didn't think he would come near her bedroom. And, if he did, she had no intention of taunting him, as storybook heroines sometimes did, by enticing and then rejecting a would-be lover.

No, the nightgown was a silly, irrational purchase and she had pushed it to the bottom of her suitcase, fearing if she left it behind Anna would find it. She knew Brent wouldn't come near her, for several reasons, but chiefly because if there were no repercussions from the first time he had made love to her, he wouldn't wish for any further complications which might prevent him getting rid of her as soon as possible.

She had felt a little humiliated, when Frank had asked, at not knowing either the time or place she was going to be married. Brent hadn't rung. She had thought he might, but when he didn't she produced what she hoped was a plausible explanation about the extra work he had to get through in order to get away for a honeymoon. Brent hadn't mentioned a honeymoon and her voice had choked over it, but Frank hadn't appeared to notice. Sari's mouth, as they drove towards London, twisted wryly. Frank had noticed little since Brent had offered him Carnford. His head appeared to be forever in clouds of calculations as his future suddenly presented the most exciting challenge of his life. A wife, a place of his own—if there were a few drawbacks he didn't see them. Who would, Sari thought, in his position?

Again Brent's astuteness struck her bitterly. He had known exactly how to divert Frank and safeguard his own interests at the same time. Now Frank was his willing slave, entirely won over. Even a divorce might find Frank still on his side. After all, who was going to fall out with someone whom Frank had once described as a man who not only supplied bread and butter but jam as well!

Brent had refused to allow them to spend the night in a hotel, or with Cilla. He had instructed Frank to come straight to his house in Holland Park. His staff had their instructions and he would join them in time for dinner.

Sari wasn't certain she cared for the idea of them all being crowded together in accommodation where she might have to share a room with Lydia. Lydia wasn't the trouble, it was herself. Since that fateful night at Carnford she hadn't been able to sleep properly and often spent hours wandering around her room suffering from spells of uncontrollable weeping. During the day her unhappiness was something she had managed to hide, but she had no defence against dreams that woke her to a raw misery she had no desire for Lydia to witness.

Brent's house was an unexpected revelation, making her realise for the first time just how very affluent he must be. It was a superb double-fronted structure, standing in a broad, tree-lined street, and inside were many rooms, all elegantly furnished. A manservant called Carter let them in and introduced his wife as Brent's housekeeper. A maid, formally dressed, hovered in the background, and Carter informed them that the chauffeur, who was out at the moment with Mr Holding, completed a staff of four. When Sari thought of Brent cooking their meals and helping her sort out her aunt's furniture in Cornwall, she almost gasped.

If the house was a surprise to Sari, their first sight of their master's slender young fiancée, with her riot of blazing silky curls and green cat's eyes which seemed forever threatening to take over her face must have had a similar effect on his staff, but, like all perfectly trained servants, they didn't betray anything. Mrs Carter, kindly and middle-aged, showed Lydia and Frank to their rooms, then took Sari to hers.

There had been a little confusion to begin with when Lydia, with her confidence and undoubted sophistication, had been mistaken for Brent's bride-to-be. Even now Mrs Carter's eyes rested on Sari with faint bewilderment, making Sari wonder despairingly just how unsuitable she thought she was.

'Tea will be served in the lounge in half an hour, miss,' she said, as she departed, leaving Sari alone in a luxurious bedroom with bathroom attached.

Sari wandered aimlessly for a few minutes trying to recover her breath, then she washed her hands and began to unpack. Mrs Carter had assured her that Polly, the maid, would do this while she was having tea, but Sari decided to do it herself. Carefully she hung her wedding outfit away before going to join the others in the lounge.

The lounge was large and comfortable, and for the next hour she sat with Frank and Lydia, watching TV and drinking tea. Lydia did most of the talking. She was impressed by everything and didn't try to hide the fact.

'You're a lucky girl!' she said to Sari, and continued on this theme until Frank began looking a trifle impatient and suggested it was time to change, if they weren't to keep Brent waiting. Brent had apparently telephoned to enquire if they had arrived and had left a message that he was taking them out to dinner.

'We've well over an hour yet,' Sari protested, preferring Lydia's chattering tongue to her own company.

'You two will probably find you need it,' said Frank dryly'

Sari had showered but not dressed when there was a knock on her door. 'Come in,' she called, believing it to be the maid.

It wasn't. It was Brent. He stepped inside, closing the door behind him. As it was his house, she might have expected him, so she didn't know why she should feel so startled. Her heart jumped right into her throat as she stared at him, and she was relieved that he didn't attempt to touch her.

'Hello. Have you settled in?' he asked almost formally, his eyes going slowly over her.

Although he kept his distance she felt the coolness of his searching glance on the deeply shadowed cleft between her breasts and flushed. 'Yes, thank you,' she drew the belt of her thin robe tighter, 'only just.'

'You like it?'

'Who wouldn't?' she shrugged. Then, as the coolness she strove for deserted her, she attacked him wildly. 'Brent, you realise your staff will probably despise me! I've had no experience in running a house this size.'

'You seemed to cope well enough at Carnford,' he pointed out patiently, his eyes not straying. 'You managed Anna beautifully.'

'But the Carters might be different!' she exclaimed, all but stamping her foot.

'You're marrying me, not my staff,' he replied curtly. 'Sari, for God's sake! If you like I'll sack the lot, if it will make you any happier.'

'Oh, no—please! I'm sorry, Brent. It's the last thing I would ask you to do . . .'

'Sari?' He moved suddenly before she could retreat, taking her burnished head in his two hands. With his grey eyes staring down into hers, he murmured softly, 'Don't you realise how lovely you are? I like you as you are, and in a few months, no doubt some famous hairdresser and some equally famous couturier will have turned you into a raving beauty. The lines, the elegance, the shape is all there, and so also is the breeding, which would enable you to cope with dozens of servants, let alone my few. So stop worrying!'

His lengthy, decisive speech took her breath away so thoroughly that she could only gaze at him, her green eyes, set like jewels in a perfect skin, far more tempting than she knew. With a hollow groan Brent bent his head to take control of a trembling pink mouth. Sari's whole body felt it was going a little mad as their lips joined with a force of passion that sent sharp spears of desire darting right through her.

It was strange how, whenever she was near him, the

world seemed to float away. She tried to keep her lips closed, but a fiery warmth parted them. His breath was coming harshly, she could hear it, just as she could feel him becoming fully aroused and trembling against her.

Hating herself, because when she had been innocent she hadn't been aware of such things, she began struggling. But before she could break free the bedroom door was suddenly flung open, shattering them apart. Sari tried numbly to draw the fronts of her robe together as her dazed eyes encountered a furious Santo.

'So this is where you are—what's going on?' he cried, his young face as flushed as Sari's as he glared at her accusingly. 'It didn't take you long, did it? And you, dear uncle!' he stressed at Brent. 'My God, you couldn't wait to get me out of the way, could you! Carter tells me you're going to be married.'

A stunned Sari fully expected Brent to be furious, but instead he retained his hold on her arm and though he regarded his nephew narrowly for a moment, he merely said quietly, 'You'd better close the door, Santo, unless you want everyone to know you've lost your temper.'

Santo, clearly incensed, obeyed literally, crashing his whole weight against it as he shouted, 'Do you think I care? Haven't I a right to be mad after what you've done?' he glowered at Brent. 'She belonged to me and you stole her!'

'I—I never belonged to you, Santo,' Sari managed to get a word in weakly, feeling she was going crazy.

'She was never yours, Santo.' Brent's voice was steel-edged.

'You seem very sure!' Santo jeered.

'I am!' Brent was unexpectedly emphatic.

'My God!' Santo raged, 'just what has been going on? Have you already ravished her? Well, you can have her, the frigid little bitch! For all your boast, I doubt if you got any further than I did.'

He got no further than that. Brent, white with anger, shook him like a dog, disregarding Sari's frantic cries. He was bigger than Santo. Sari saw how Santo looked a mere boy beside him, and desperately she clutched at Brent's arm, begging him to stop.

'Oh, please,' she whispered, as he did so, 'please don't fight over me. Santo——' she began, distractedly thinking of telling him about the divorce.

Brent must have known what was on her mind and cut in curtly, 'It's true, Santo, Sari and I are to be married tomorrow.' He let go of Santo as abruptly as he had taken hold of him, but as Santo sank palely into the nearest chair, he stood over him, a little anger still on his face. 'You're welcome to attend the wedding or stay away, but whatever you decide, I will not tolerate any more scenes.'

Santo, looking thoroughly shaken, appealed to Sari, who felt dreadful. 'I tried to see you. I rang Frank and he told me you'd left Carnford. He didn't know how long you would be away. I was going to wait until you came back.'

'You were so much in love you didn't think it was worth going to check?' Brent intervened sarcastically.

'I had no reason to doubt her brother's word,' Santo muttered huffily.

'He wasn't telling a lie.' Sari stared at Brent resentfully. 'I wasn't there, and Frank would have thought you were mad if you'd gone all that way just to check.' She forgot Frank had said Brent had been there several times, almost turning the place upside down in his efforts to find her.

Santo sighed, rubbing the sweat from his brow, with every appearance of a young man feeling increasingly martyred. He gazed at Sari, ignoring Brent.

'I'm sorry I said you were frigid, Sari. I'm sorrier still I didn't tell you I loved you until the day I left Carnford, but you didn't give me any encouragement. My uncle might appear to be the better bet, but he won't love you half as much as I do.'

Seeing Brent's simmering anger again reach boiling point, Sari feared another explosion, and was relieved that he managed to control himself. His eyes glittered, but he spoke almost flatly. 'I'm not as willing as you to air my feelings in public, Santo, but I won't allow you to judge the depth of them—or Sari's either. She doesn't love you, that you can believe, and if you were really honest, you would admit the overriding passion in your life is defying me!'

'Because you never treat me as a grown man!' Santo muttered sullenly.

'I will,' Brent returned grimly, 'when you begin acting like one. Then,' he added cynically, 'I'll be only too glad to. For years, since your father died, I've carried on as though you'd taken his place as my full partner. You've had every penny he would have been entitled to without having to lift a finger. I'm even willing to wait until you stop playing round and decide whether to step into his shoes or sell out, but I certainly won't tolerate your trying to take over my bride—now or ever!'

Sari couldn't get Brent's last two words out of her head, throughout the long evening that followed, or all the next day, from her wakening moment, through the wedding ceremony, to the minute their plane touched down in Singapore, which he had chosen for their honeymoon.

Santo had come to the wedding, after all, a very subdued Santo, looking as if Brent's lecture had thoroughly shaken him. The scene in her bedroom had shaken Sari as well, though it had filled in gaps she had wondered about. Secretly she agreed with Brent's caustic conclusions that if Santo had really loved her he would have gone to Carnford personally to make sure Frank had been speaking the truth. She didn't believe that Santo had ever been much more than fond of her. Probably she was the first girl he had ever spent as long as six weeks with and had merely clung to her because his emotions were still adolescent for his age. Maybe one day he would grow up, she might even be able to help him, once he had had time to get over his infatuation. Meanwhile, although his pale, resentful face continued to worry her, she didn't dare tell him the truth about Brent and herself.

After Brent had ruthlessly dismissed Santo from her room, he had recalled how she had very nearly said too much and warned her to be more careful in future.

'Santo may be lazy, but he isn't slow to pick things up,' he had said grimly.

'I'm sorry,' Sari had apologised bitterly, 'but don't worry, I'll try and remember not to say or do anything which might hurt your dignity. After all, I owe you a lot, don't I? Plenty of men leave the girl in the lurch, but you're going to marry me.'

She had been startled by the grimness of his expression, the cold unhappiness she had imagined she had seen for a moment in his eyes. But he had merely shrugged and left her after requesting her to be ready in fifteen minutes.

CHAPTER NINE

BRENT had asked no one to the wedding apart from an elderly aunt, who lived in London, and his best man and his wife.

'It was a case of asking dozens—maybe hundreds, or none at all,' he said, when Sari expressed surprise. 'But don't worry, we won't really escape. Most of my friends will be demanding to meet you when we return from our honeymoon. We'll probably be bombarded with invitations to dinner parties, and expected to give some too.'

On the morning of their wedding she hadn't seen him. He might have been tactfully honouring old superstitions by keeping out of the way, but whatever his reasons she had been glad of the brief respite after the tension of the evening before.

Mrs Carter had brought her breakfast to bed and Lydia had helped her to dress. The creamy silk dress with its matching jacket looked wonderful against Sari's pale, perfect skin, while a small hat and froth of a veil nestled lovingly on the burnished brightness of her hair. Lydia had achieved miracles, Sari was sure, with her face and hair. Otherwise, she thought, glancing dazedly in a mirror before they left, how could she have looked such a vision of loveliness?

Throughout the rest of the day, from the moment she arrived at his side in the register office, Brent acted as if he loved her. Sari, although she managed to smile quite frequently, couldn't match his performance, but was comforted by the fact that it was well known that brides were often too overcome by nerves to be radiant.

Brent's aunt, an elderly dowager, of much the same calibre as Aunt Joan, was disapproving of the brief civil

service, and at the reception in Brent's home, she
tackled Sari. She seemed frighteningly determined to
discover why they had been in such a hurry.

'I know once Brent makes up his mind there's no
stopping him, but surely marriage shouldn't be treated
in the same way as business merger. Mind you,' she had
added dryly, 'marriage today seems to be regarded as
more of a sex merger than a love affair, considering the
haste of the divorce which often follows.'

Another time Sari might have been faintly amused by
such frankness from a lady of such obviously advanced
age and moral principles, but Miss Holding's slightly
cynical views applied too closely to Sari's own
circumstances to be any way comfortable. Fortunately
her painful flush was taken for maidenly modesty,
rather than embarrassment, and Miss Holding flowed
regardlessly on.

'Brent really ought to have considered you, my dear
child. You would have graced our old family church
wonderfully, in white satin and lace, of course. Didn't
he allow you any say in the matter?'

'No, I'm afraid I didn't,' Brent's voice came between
them as Sari was searching nervously for hers. 'I confess
I was impatient. In this,' he murmured, half under his
breath, 'more than I've ever been about anything else in
my life.'

Sari had a suspicion that he wasn't talking about
their actual wedding, but his aunt, only catching odd
words, eyed him through her lorgnette with forgiving
adoration.

'Oh, well,' she shrugged her elderly but still elegant
shoulders, 'you never got where you are today by
practising procrastination. But don't hurry your bride
too much, Brent. She's a charming girl and I'm sure
you'll find she's worth the trouble.'

'What did you think of the advice my aunt gave me?'
Brent asked idly on the plane which was taking them
from Singapore to Penang, where a friend of his had

loaned them his house for two weeks.

Sari, unprepared for his query, frowned. Why, when they had already spent three days in Singapore, had he never mentioned it until now? She wished he hadn't. She saw he was watching her closely and the panicky feelings she recognised too clearly returned to her breast. The relative tranquillity she had thought she had achieved since their wedding seemed to drop away from her, into the gem-like beauty of the Straits of Malacca over which they were flying.

'It—it's the prerogative, isn't it, of elderly ladies to give advice,' she replied eventually, trying to speak lightly. 'At your aunt's age I don't suppose you need seek it any more.'

'You haven't answered my question,' Brent said harshly, when she had expected he might be amused.

This time she didn't attempt to evade the issue. 'It probably came too late,' she remarked bleakly. 'But do we have to talk about it?'

'We have to talk about it some time,' he said bluntly.

Sari stirred, her alarmed, fluttering glance turning from his unreadable grey one. They were flying through blue skies, the odd milky-white cloud. Everywhere the colours were vivid, by Northern European standards, almost exaggerated, but the brilliance of the sun gave everything a dreamlike quality. She had felt the magic of it in Singapore, and she had found Singapore amazing enough to take her mind, if not completely, then partly off the troubles which had haunted her in England.

She had began thinking this was why Brent had taken her there. But if so, why had he returned deliberately to a subject which he must know filled her with apprehension? She didn't want to talk about the reason they had had to get married, or of their divorce, in a year's time.

In Singapore they had stayed in a huge, breathtaking hotel. The sheer wealth and luxury of it she had found truly amazing. It had six restaurants, one revolving, from which they had been able to see Singapore, Malaysia and Indonesia. There had been a coffee shop open twenty-four hours a day and a night club and discothèque and swimming pool forming just a few of the available amenities.

Their suite had been large enough to accommodate them without embarrassment, and although Sari had become used to seeing Brent wandering round in a short robe, he had never come near her. Now he was coming near, if in a different way, and she wondered apprehensively why.

'Please,' she whispered, hoping if she begged for time he might forget again, 'can't it wait?'

'If you like,' he said tersely.

Hearing no promise in his voice that he would be willing to postpone the subject indefinitely, she went pale, whereas before her cheeks had been tinted with healthy colour. 'I thought we were coming here to enjoy ourselves, not talk,' she muttered.

He stared into her face and said savagely, 'That's an idea.'

She shivered, her eyes daring no farther than his powerful jaw and firm mouth, which had gone curiously white. She had no desire to meet the cool levelness of his gaze that could pierce her so disconcertingly. Why had his mood changed from the casual friendliness he had shown her since they left England? Wearily she closed her eyes and tried to relax, but the bewilderment forever churning through her head refused to let her.

It was only one hour's flight from Singapore to Penang. Soon they had landed and were on their way to their final destination. Sari hadn't asked any questions about Brent's friend or his house, but as she began to be aware of the sheer loveliness of the island she became curious.

'Does your friend live here all the year round?' she asked.

'Yes.' Brent was giving most of his attention to the car he had hired at the airport. 'He and his wife, Julie.'

'Oh, you didn't say he was married.'

'You didn't ask.'

No, she hadn't. Nervously she lapsed into silence again. The car was small, and his muscular thigh brushed hers, making her flinch. It was a purely involuntary movement, a reaction from the sharp surge of sensation that shot through her as their limbs touched. She hoped he hadn't noticed, but a quick glance at his tight-lipped face made her suspect he had.

To avoid making more mistakes, destined to annoy him, she tried to remember exactly what he had told her about their honeymoon. While they had been discussing it he had said that November wasn't the best time for touring Europe. When she had suggested they stayed in England, he had shaken his head. The intimacy of his country place, with toasted crumpets in front of a cosy fire, hadn't appealed to him. He had also been adamant about remaining in London under the curious if discreet eyes of his staff. Then he had surprised her by revealing that it had been as he was considering the merits of the various resorts he knew in other parts of the world that a friend of his had rung and subsequently offered them his villa in Penang.

Brent hadn't mentioned their honeymoon until the eve of their wedding, and, after the row with Santo, Sari's nerves hadn't been at their best. It had angered her, although she had tried not to show it, that Brent should ask her advice over something he had already arranged. She must have taken offence, but as she didn't usually sulk, she couldn't understand why she hadn't asked for more details since.

In an effort to put things right, and to ease the tension which always seemed to spring up between them if they got too close, she enquired hastily, 'What does your friend do? He must be a writer or something like that. I might have been able to guess if you'd told me his name. Perhaps,' she added, searching for inspiration, 'he's a botanist.'

Brent's brows rose sardonically on her flushed cheeks and tumbled speech. 'His name is Ogman, James Ogman, and he's a writer. You were right first time. His stories usually have an Oriental background. Maybe you've read some of his thrillers or travel books?'

'No,' Sari pondered, then shook her head, 'I can't say I have.'

'No? He's quite well known.'

'Oh, yes,' Sari agreed quickly, 'I didn't mean I hadn't heard of him—it's just that thrillers aren't exactly my scene. I like travel books, though. I wonder if he's left any lying around I can read——'

'Well, anyway,' Brent went on, 'he lives here most of the year. He and Julie fell in love with Penang years ago. They usually spend about a month each year in London, visiting James's publisher and looking up old friends, and doing, of all things, their Christmas shopping. They'd only been there a day or two when he rang me and we all had lunch together. That was when he offered me the house.'

'It was very good of them,' Sari commented.

'We'll see, won't we?' Brent replied enigmatically.

Sari hadn't known quite what to expect, but from her very first sight of the spacious villa she loved it. It was easy to see, she thought wryly, that James Ogman wasn't one of the world's poorest writers! The setting was superb, a beautiful, palm-fringed bay with an azure sea and sky, and a beach so smooth and clean it would be easy to believe it had never known the imprint of a human foot.

Inside the villa, the rooms were large and airy, and there were plenty of them. Sari liked the lounge with its Chinese ivory and Indonesian woodcarvings and Malaysian pewterware. The Malayan couple, who spoke good English and who were to come in through the day to look after them, showed them the spare bedrooms and left them to choose for themselves.

As they all seemed much the same, spacious with white rugs on the floor and wide double beds, Sari chose at random, and while Brent departed with the servants to consult about meals, she changed quickly into a bikini and beach robe and went outside.

Outside, the air was beautiful—and warm, but while the sea beckoned she wasn't sure if it was safe to swim. It might be wiser to ask Brent first. She wasn't even sure about the beach, whether they were at liberty to go where they liked or not, but as he had been here before he must know. With a sigh she sat down in one of the many chairs on the terrace, which ran the full length of the house, to wait for him.

When she heard him coming her stomach muscles tightened as she realised this would be the first time she had been alone with him since leaving London. In Singapore they had spent their days sightseeing and the evenings in popular nightspots, from which they had rarely returned before dawn. Brent took a chair nearby and as Sari turned her head to look at him her breath caught. He had discarded his clothes too, in favour of a pair of swimming trunks, and this was the first time she had seen him with so little on. On a certain night which she still refused to think about, it had been too dark to see clearly. A slow flush burned her cheeks and her heart beat rapidly as her eyes seemed unaccountably fixed on Brent's tall, well muscled body. The powerful masculinity he emanated jolted her to an uneasy awareness of what she might be up against in her efforts to remain immune from him.

As though he in no way objected to the attention he was receiving, he smiled at her. 'Do you think you're going to like it here?'

His voice broke the trance she was in, enough, to allow her to avert her dazed glance. 'It—it's very beautiful.'

A trace of mockery touched his mouth. 'You sound rather doubtful! Don't tell me you're looking for the serpent in our garden of Eden already?'

'Maybe I don't have to look far,' she snapped, determined to rally her defences rather than commit the fatal mistake of smiling back at him. If he expected her to do that, he expected too much, she raged silently, and the sooner he realised it the better.

As if aware of the inner storm shaking her, Brent reclined in his chair and infuriatingly closed his eyes. Well, let him, Sari continued to rage wildly, she had no desire for either his company or conversation! After a few minutes she grew contrarily tired of being ignored and asked tentatively,

'I've been wondering what you'll find to do all day.'

'Me?' He opened grey eyes a slit to look at her. 'Lounge in the sun, I should think. The last few weeks have been rather hectic, and Singapore wasn't exactly restful.'

'I suppose I can swim and tour the island while you're resting,' she remarked sarcastically. 'I'd like to go home with a gorgeous tan.'

'You'll never get one unless you take something off.' He closed one eye again but left the other cynically on her beach robe.

Defiantly her hands flew to the tie at her waist, only to discover she had knotted it so tightly in her hurry to escape the bedroom that she couldn't manage to undo it.

'Blast and damn!' she muttered under her breath.

'Tut, tut, remember my delicate ears!' Brent's brows rose but he was beside her in a flash. 'Here, let me.' His fingers, stronger by far than hers, dealt nimbly with the stubborn sash.

His voice grated. 'Just what the hell were you trying to prove—or keep at bay—when you tied that?'

What about her ears? 'I didn't realise,' she faltered, as he began slipping the towelling robe from her shoulders. 'It's an easy enough thing to do!'

'Is it?'

Startled, Sari realised his voice had thickened slightly as he flung the robe aside and stared down at her. As his glance slid over the slenderness of her perfectly curved body she felt herself cringe. She had no intention of enticing him. Yes, she wanted revenge, but not this way, for it would mean she would have to reject him, and she never could feel confident she would be able to. While it might be a bitter pill to swallow, she never allowed herself to underestimate the power Brent had over her. She ought never to have worn a bikini which left her almost indecently bare, but how on earth did his mere gaze manage to shake her so terribly?

She hadn't been aware of holding her breath until he abruptly turned from her and she heard it leave her throat in a rush that left her trembling.

'I'm going for a swim before lunch.' His voice sounded normal again. 'You'd better watch the sun on that skin. There's plenty of lotion in the bathroom, I noticed, if you didn't bring any with you.'

'Let me come too,' Sari begged, suddenly forgetting her animosity at the prospect of a dip in such a wonderful-looking sea. 'Oh, please, Brent!' She jumped up to race after him, catching his arm just as he was shaking his dark head and stepping from the terrace. Eagerly she raised excited green eyes to his face. 'I used to swim all the time in Cornwall!'

'Yes,' a nerve jerked at the side of his mouth as his eyes fell from hers to the small but perfect hand clutching his wrist, 'that may be so, but have you recovered sufficiently from Cornwall? We don't want you running any risks, do we?'

Was he, for some reason, taunting her? Sari let go of his arm as though stung, her face paling. 'If you're talking about your son and heir,' she cried, suddenly driven beyond discretion, 'I—I don't believe there's going to be one!'

'I wouldn't be so sure,' he drawled coldly, his eyes resting intently on the full swell of her breasts.

'Oh!' She flushed scarlet, hating him, and herself, for the astonishing surge of feeling that rushed through her. 'I don't care what you think,' she muttered defiantly, 'but I'm sure a short swim won't hurt me, whatever my condition. I swam all the year round in Cornwall. It's not as if I wasn't used to it.'

'Come on then,' he gave in, but with his hard face filled with such harshness as to make her wish uneasily that she hadn't insisted on having her own way.

Brent was a much more powerful swimmer than she was, although she didn't try and compete. Rather than risk renewing his anger or spoiling his pleasure, she contented herself with staying fairly close inshore. She had no wish to try and prove anything, and his comments before they entered the water had shaken her, making her decide it might be best to keep a low profile for a while.

After lunch, the Malayan couple departed for their own house along the beach. Apparently they had intended returning to cook dinner, but Brent had told them that he and Sari would be dining out.

'We can eat in town,' he explained to Sari moodily after they had gone. 'It will make a change for you.'

Sari would sooner have stayed where she was, even if it had meant cooking their own supper. The last few days, while exciting, had tired her, and hadn't Brent confessed to being tired too? Apart from this, she had taken quite a liking to Chinese food and would have loved to have done a little experimenting. Perhaps the Malayan couple wouldn't want her meddling in their kitchen, though, which might be just as well, she thought with a wry flicker of humour, taking sudden pity on Brent's stomach.

After lunch he disappeared in the room he had seemingly chosen for his own, and when he didn't come out she decided he must be having a nap. He looked very tired. Sari gazed at his closed door with a frown that was more anxious than she was aware of. Despite the implacable exterior he usually presented, occasionally, when she had caught him off guard, she had been startled by a certain greyness in his face which made her heart contract and caused her to wonder if their brief marriage was already proving as much a strain for him as it was for her.

Unable to settle in the house with Brent so close yet distant, she decided to take advantage of the short respite his absence gave her and return to the beach. Hunting around, she found something to lie on and quickly slipped from the house. It might be wiser not to go about half naked when he was there, but she was determined to get a tan. She wasn't sure about her face. Her creamy skin usually refused to change colour, but it had never been exposed to sunshine like this before. With no sign of anyone stirring in the house, she undid the top of her bikini and stretched out.

The effects of the sun and sea were soporific. Soon she began dozing as the sun poured over her and the sound of the waves breaking gently on the shore was like a lullaby. She heard no sound and felt impatient when her eyes flickered open, but she knew immediately that Brent was there.

She waited a moment, as her eyes caught a slight movement, then tensed as her glance lifted a few inches up the length of a powerful leg. He must be standing with his legs apart, as she could only see one. Hastily she closed her eyes again, hoping he hadn't noticed the startled flutter of her lashes, unaware that both that and the quickening of her breath had clearly betrayed her.

'Sari!' She knew she could no longer pretend she was sleeping when he spoke, but she wondered at the grimness of his voice. 'What did I tell you,' he snapped, 'about using a suntan lotion?'

'I'm only staying out a few minutes,' she muttered, trying desperately to wriggle her hands around her back to refasten her bikini.

Silently Brent watched her futile struggles, then he dropped down beside her. 'Lie still,' he commanded curtly. 'You don't have to sit up or turn over. I've brought something with me.'

Sari had no other option but to obey. If she jumped up she suspected she might lose her top altogether. 'I thought you were sleeping.' Her voice was muffled as she pressed tightly into the rug.

'I might have done if I'd had company, eventually,' he replied heavily.

A cool blob of lotion landed between her shoulder-blades, with his hands dispersing it in gliding movements going gently over her. He used pressure lightly, as though not to frighten her, but as always she had to brace herself against an avalanche of feeling. At his touch all her bones and muscles seemed to be turning to jelly. The overwhelming sensation jerked her head up, before she realised what she was doing, and their eyes met.

Brent didn't move. It was a crazy sensation, lasting no longer than a few seconds. He was sitting back, only touching her with his fingertips, yet she felt he had come suffocatingly close. She swallowed and had to close her lids against the smouldering darkness of his glance as it began going slowly over her.

Her tongue moistening her lips nervously, she cast around in her tormented mind wildly for anything that might give her dwindling resistance a boost. 'You should have married someone like Gloria de Courcy, instead of me!' she gasped.

'Gloria?' he had resumed his self-appointed task with the lotion, but paused. 'I believe she's in the States.'

'Did you ... do you love her very much?' Sari got out rawly.

He sounded sardonically amused. 'Whatever gave

you that impression?'

'You couldn't have been responsible, could you?' Sari choked. 'You brought her to Carnford. We thought you were lovers.'

'We?'

Sari hated the faint amusement in his voice and was forced to confess reluctantly, 'Well, when you first arrived, Frank did wonder . . .'

Brent paused again. 'We were never lovers, although,' he admitted, 'I had taken her out occasionally. That she came to Carnford with me was more of a coincidence than anything else. I happened to be at the party given for the cast, the night her play closed down. She was pretty low, and when I said I was going to be out of town, she practically begged to come with me. I don't believe she ever imagined I would take her suggestion seriously. And I didn't,' he added cynically, 'until I conceived a suddenly brilliant notion that she might be useful as a kind of protective façade from behind which I might safely view the dangerous young siren who was trying to seduce my nephew!'

Sari couldn't imagine Brent hiding behind any woman and noted suspiciously. 'She didn't stay long.'

'No,' Brent answered wryly, 'I took one look at you and didn't want her there any more. The reason wasn't clear immediately, but I sent her away.'

While frowning at such ruthlessness, Sari was unable to prevent herself from asking tentatively, 'So you didn't have an affair?'

'No,' he said, very decisively. 'I had only to be with Gloria a day to realise she left me cold. And then I met you,' his hands tensed in fists on her smooth skin, 'and I couldn't think of anyone else, damn you!'

It sounded so much of an insult, Sari was able to retort coldly, 'But you just wanted me!'

'And that wasn't enough?'

Did he have to sound so savage? She was glad it was her back he was rubbing so he wouldn't know how fast her heart was beating. 'It's pretty basic, isn't it?' she muttered disparagingly.

'Wanting, loving,' he muttered back, 'isn't one just a part of the other? But you don't have to tell me I made a mess of things at Carnford. I know.'

Did he mean for her, or himself?

Because Sari wasn't sure, she hesitated, and Brent must have taken her silence for agreement, because he sighed deeply and continued rubbing cream in her back. Then his hands slipped to her waist, to curve the smooth bareness of her hips before moving gently upwards to span her narrow ribcage. Could sunburn, she wondered, cause her any more pain than the trails of heat Brent's hands were generating?

'Please,' she whispered, making a breathless effort to twist free of him, 'that's enough!'

'It may be for you,' he replied thickly, suddenly, without warning turning her over a little less gently.

Her startled eyes wavered on his darkly flushed face as he knelt above her, and a tremor ran through her as she flattened herself against the rug, her hands digging tensely in the sand at either side of her. She felt like a trapped animal. 'Will you leave me alone!' she whispered huskily. 'You promised!'

Brent's eyes narrowed as he shook his head. 'What's one more transgression to a condemned man? Maybe I've left you alone too long.'

Then he lowered himself beside her, the hard toughness of his thighs moving against hers to hold her immobile as he kissed her in a way that made her senses reel. His mouth was sweetly savage and she could feel the blood rushing and pounding in her ears as she recognised his power over her, but she tried not to cling to him.

As though scorning her attempted rejection and determined to make her repudiate it, he slid his long fingers under her bikini top, pulling it away from her. Softly, as she began quivering helplessly, he explored the pale hollows of her throat and neck, while all the time his eyes feasting on the bare, taut curves of her breasts.

Sari's heart was beating so loudly she feared he might hear it as his teeth nipped her tender flesh and his hands caressed until her entire body began aching with desire. Then his arms went under her to raise her to him and his tongue licked and tormented her hardened nipples until her breath became painful gasps and her fingers dug convulsively in his thick dark hair as she pressed herself urgently to him. She felt small and of no account as her hands clutched and clung to his broad shoulders and she became aware of the heat in the limbs moving over hers with a savage intensity. As their bodies melted together she met the ruthlessness of his passion with a matching need of her own and was both deaf and blind to everything but the searing flame which threatened to engulf them.

It came as a shock, just as she was expecting the heavens to open, to find herself released instead. Suddenly Brent was thrusting her away, jumping to his feet. If her eyes could have penetrated the mist that swam briefly before her, she still couldn't have seen his face as he abruptly turned his back on her.

'I could have taken you,' his voice came so roughly she scarcely recognised it, 'but I must be a coward in spite of my brave words. I don't think I could face your increased hatred afterwards. It's enough to put up with as it is.'

Sari gulped, her whole body crying out for release, for what she couldn't have. How easy it would be to accept what Brent offered—if she could forget the past, and the divorce in a year's time. He might want to make love to her, but he still wanted a divorce. Hadn't he frequently reminded her of it? Which proved he had no intention of having her for his wife permanently. He would use and discard her. How could she have been crazy enough to forget that, as well as the way he had already treated her?

Unhappily, her eyes green as emeralds, she stared dully at his tall, powerfully built figure. She felt harassed and inadequate, while Brent seemed hard and formidable, and—reproving! 'You can't accuse me of encouraging you,' she choked.

'No, that's true,' he swung round again, his face drawn, 'I didn't mean to take advantage, but you're very desirable. Maybe the situation took advantage of me.'

Meeting the self-derision in his glance, Sari tried not to shiver. She had to pretend to be calm while inwardly she trembled so much she didn't dare get up. If his emotions were confused, it could be nothing to the state hers were in! She had to have time to rethink, but how could she do that with Brent standing over her, tempting her to fling herself in his arms and never think again.

'Sari' his voice broke through her tormented thoughts dryly, 'would you mind fixing your bikini? It isn't helping, the way it is now.'

Sari went red with embarrassment as she suddenly realised she was practically bare from the waist up. 'I'm sorry,' she mumbled stiffly, her fingers all thumbs.

He didn't offer to help. 'I'm going to swim again. Want to come?'

There was no warmth in his invitation, but he appeared too tense to do more than let the words slip curtly out.

'It might be a good idea,' she nodded, 'but you go ahead.'

The buoyancy of the water gave a slight lift to her spirits when she joined him. She even managed a faint smile that unconsciously held an element of pleading. It was comforting to find he had waited for her, which she decided he wouldn't have done if he had still been annoyed with her. Not that he had any right to be annoyed with her, she reminded herself quickly. She was the injured party, wasn't she? It might be easier to meet him halfway until they returned to London, though. Then she needn't see any more of him than was absolutely necessary.

Later, after they had showered and dressed, she again felt like telling him she would rather stay in, but common sense prevailed. The strain of their relationship was bound to be less if they went out occasionally.

As she was frowning pensively, wishing she had left the beach earlier and not missed the opportunity of getting herself sorted out, Brent watched her narrowly. This evening he was wearing a white dinner jacket with a pleated shirt and he looked arrogantly arresting.

'Why the frown?' he jeered tautly, his eyes going over her, from the top of her shining, silky head to the slender straps of silver sandals peeping out below the long, frothy skirt of her beautiful pale blue dress. 'Don't tell me you'd like to send me out to dine alone! I had hoped my company was beginning to have some appeal.'

Why did his moods change so? Sari raised startled eyes to meet the derisive mockery in his face. 'I think you're jumping to the wrong conclusions,' she replied, trying to speak calmly. 'I'm looking forward to going out. It—it isn't as if ours is a normal honeymoon.'

'That was your choice.' He strode to the window, the whole breadth of his shoulders tense. 'But if you're determined to see the sights, perhaps it's just as well. If ours had been a normal honeymoon, as you put it, you'd have been lucky to have got farther than the bedroom. Now go on,' his hands clenched, 'accuse me of acting out of character.'

'I—I don't remember you being over-dramatic,' she faltered, the effort to slow down her heartbeats so enervating she scarcely knew what she was saying.

'No,' Brent's breath came heavily as he turned to stare at her broodingly, 'I never used to be, but you're like a fever in my blood. If you don't want me there's as sure as hell got to be an antidote!'

Sari didn't reply, having no idea how to deal with such savage bitterness. They couldn't put back the clock and they were both being torn apart in different ways. She was relieved when Brent suggested grimly that they left immediately. It seemed he wished for the intimacy of a shared drink before they left no more than she did.

She thought George Town, the busy port-city on the island's north-east corner, noisy but attractive. Brent said it was well worth exploring and promised to bring her back for a good look around before they went home. Having been here previously, he knew the best places to eat, and the restaurant he chose had an amazing selection of both Eastern and Western dishes. They ate well, if not happily—but then she could scarcely blame a restaurant for her own personal troubles, Sari thought bitterly.

CHAPTER TEN

THE mounting tension between Brent and herself was so strong it almost frightened Sari, and she was greatly relieved when, eventually, they returned to the villa and she was back in her own room again. Her relationship with Brent appeared to be growing worse instead of better, and she had no idea what to do about it.

She didn't love Brent. As she took a shower she desperately tried to convince herself that love need have nothing to do with the desire which constantly threatened to consume her. Would it make any difference, she wondered, if she gave herself to him once? Might it not cure the awful hunger that ignoring him only seemed to increase? What had she to lose anyway? Hadn't she already lost that which she could never have to lose again?

Her head reeling from the effects of the wine she had swallowed rather recklessly during dinner, she felt suddenly suffocated in the house. If she sat for a while on the terrace, where the air, at this hour of night, was clear and cool, it might be possible to work something out. There might be no easy answer to her problems, but at least the air might make her feel better.

After drying quickly, she donned a thin robe, but as she ran outside, to her dismay she stumbled straight into Brent's arms. He was passing her door and automatically his arms came up to catch her as she fell helplessly against him.

He was as lightly dressed as she was. Her face encountered the roughness of his chest, where his robe parted from the loosely tied cord at his waist, and immediately her nostrils were assailed by the clean, astringent fragrance of his skin. Sari's legs nearly gave way as he affected her senses more than all the wine she had imbibed.

'Sari!' Brent made no attempt to let her go. If anything his grip tightened possessively. His voice was slightly thickened, but that could have been the bottle of whisky she had noticed him carrying to his room. 'Sari!' he groaned against her hair, something seemingly preventing him from being able to articulate more than her name.

Jerkily she moved, her lips incidentally touching his face as she raised her head. Her green eyes widened as she gazed at him in mute confusion. Her mind was advising her to flee while her heart argued in the opposite direction.

When his mouth merely brushed hers, the feather-light touch worked like magic on her already aroused senses. Suddenly she was clinging to him, her arms round his neck, inviting his full embrace. There was none of the wary reticence she had known that afternoon. The ache within her mounted until she was driven by a sweet, stabbing agony. She was giving in to the crying need within her, shamelessly and fully abandoned.

Brent's response was immediate. Sari felt it not only in the increased and hungry pressure of his mouth but in the way his whole body reacted. She could feel his hand sliding the length of her spine, holding her tightly against him until the pressure of his powerful thighs began hurting.

Only then did he release her bruised mouth, and then just enough to allow his burning glance to rove her flushed and glowing cheeks, the reflected brilliance in her eyes.

'Tell me,' he said huskily, 'that you mean this. I'm not dreaming?'

When she tried to speak but momentarily couldn't, he continued hoarsely, 'Sari, you realise what you're inviting? If you come to bed with me now anything might happen.'

His warning—and it must be one came like a shock of cold water. She had agreed to a divorce in a year's time. She had refused to dwell on the complications that would arise if there was a child to consider. Sometimes she thought she only managed to stay sane by believing she couldn't possibly be pregnant. If she gave in to Brent now and her own clamouring desires, wouldn't she be risking everything again? Unless—hope stirred tentatively—he had changed his mind about getting rid of her?

'The—the divorce?' she whispered apprehensively.

'Oh, that,' his voice was muffled and shaken as he paid more attention to the inviting hollows of her neck and ear, 'that needn't change. I realise freedom is more precious than anything else . . .'

'No!' Quickly she wrenched from his arms. 'I'm sorry, Brent, I must be going crazy! I'm sure I'm not expecting your child, and I'm certainly not going to risk it again.'

As his arms fell empty to his sides, his face appeared to turn to stone. The satisfaction and passion which had softened it was gone, the torture in his eyes swiftly veiled. 'Okay, Sari,' he nodded grimly, holding up his hand as she prepared to defend herself. 'No, I'm not about to accuse you of anything. When you flew from your room, you weren't to know I was walking past it. Another time, though, for God's sake look first. I'm only human.'

'Are you?' To rant and rave seemed all she had left. She forced her voice full of contempt. 'Sometimes I doubt it!'

Streaks of white crept along his jaw. 'You won't let me prove otherwise. You're willing to put me through hell just to satisfy a lust for revenge. Well, you can take it I'm suffering,' he muttered harshly, 'but you're quite safe as long as I believe I deserve to. And I won't stop you getting a divorce. Perhaps you won't have to even wait a whole year!'

The remainder of their honeymoon after that was a kind of quiet fiasco. Outwardly no one might have guessed they weren't enjoying themselves. Whenever anyone was around Brent acted the perfect, attentive new husband. He showed her the island. They revisited George Town and toured it in a three-wheeled trishaw, sitting up front with the bicycle rider behind. Sari was intrigued by this mode of travel and despite her heartache enjoyed it.

Brent told her that when Captain Francis Light and his crew landed at George Town two hundred years ago they found only green jungle where now there was a city of around half a million people. Primarily a Chinese town, George Town had red-tiled roofs, colonial-style buildings, ornate red-lacquered temples, old mosques and lightly travelled streets. Inside a traffic circle Sari was surprised to see a clock tower, dedicated to Queen Victoria, which seemed strangely uneasy against a background of modern high-rise buildings.

Another day they went around the coast, which was only about forty-six miles altogether. Here new hotels were springing up, and Brent said the first time he had visited the island there had been very few. He was a fund of information and they talked quite a lot, but had nothing to say to each other that other people couldn't have overheard. As time passed they became more and more like strangers, and by the middle of their second week, Sari felt so overwrought she was almost tearfully relieved when Brent suggested they cut their holiday short and went home.

'You can always come back again with your next husband,' he said cruelly. 'There are plenty of places you might stay, other than with the Ogmans.'

As if she would ever want to come back! Unhappily she took her last look at the island through eyes glazed with tears as they drove to the airport at Bayan Lepas. She would never be able to even think about Penang without recalling one of the most agonising periods of her life. As for her next husband—Brent couldn't really be serious. There would never be another one, not for her. There was no one, she admitted with painful honesty, she could ever put in his place.

In London, she was dismayed to find he expected her to take up her duties as his wife and hostess almost immediately. She might refuse to have him in her bedroom, but she soon realised he wouldn't allow her to avoid him in other ways. They would give a series of dinner parties, she was told. Their wedding had been quiet, almost secretive, and a lot of people were clamouring to meet her, people whom he wasn't anxious to offend.

Sari didn't mind the dinner parties. It gave her something to do, although all the hard work was done by the staff. Nevertheless, there was enough to take her mind partly off her own problems. It seemed ironical that she began fitting into the household so well when she would soon be leaving it. The staff liked her and made no attempt to disguise the fact. Despite Brent's frequently raised eyebrows, they ran after her, often insisting on doing things for her out of the range of their normal duties. She suspected she was being thoroughly spoiled and wondered despondently how difficult it would be to manage on her own again, after the divorce.

Whenever she thought of the divorce she felt pain, while she knew it wouldn't be as bad as it might have been if she had been pregnant. At least she had been saved the fight which would undoubtedly have arisen over a child. After nearly two months she could be quite sure she had escaped the trauma of that, and she tried to balance the regret of not having Brent's son against the assurance that one day she would be completely free of him.

He had been adamant, however, that she must live with him a whole year. He appeared to have forgotten what he had said on Penang. And while she might have run away, there was still the fear that if she did, things might go badly for Frank. Frank was increasingly busy getting established, he could well do without the repercussions any impulsive move of hers might bring down on his undeserving head.

Before they were married Brent hadn't bothered much about her clothes. Now he insisted she went to the best hairdresser and opened accounts at several stores which he ordered her to use. If she didn't he threatened to accompany her himself. Like everything else he possessed, he appeared determined that his wife should reflect his success. It might not make him happy to see her looking more desirable and well groomed each day—in fact, Sari decided, he seemed anything but happy, with his eyes usually cold and expressionless and his face drawn in deep lines, but she did detect a kind of savage satisfaction whenever he glanced at her faultless young beauty.

Not that her new, sleeker image proved much consolation to Sari. As the weeks slipped by, she sometimes felt so miserable she didn't know what to do with herself, and the effort it took to remain outwardly calm and composed became at times an intolerable strain.

Thank goodness for make-up, she sighed wryly, at the end of one particularly stressful evening as she wearily cleansed it off her face. Without the mask of foundation and powder she looked pale and haunted. Her skin was still as perfect as it had ever been, but it lacked the colour and vitality which had been one of her special features before she had been married.

This evening Brent had seemed even more terse and unapproachable than usual, and after their guests had gone he flayed her with remarks regarding her behaviour with one of his friends. Jeff Young was one of his directors and Sari had thought she was just being nice to him, but apparently she had overstepped the mark. Brent had told her grimly she could do what she liked when she was no longer his wife, but until then he refused to countenance her flirting with every man who crossed her path.

They had quarrelled fiercely—at least, Sari admitted now, she had. She had said bitter things she tried to convince herself she had meant, and now she felt so weary and disgusted with herself she only wanted to die. The sight of Brent's haggard white face, as she had finally fled from him, refused to go away.

It wasn't as though Jeff Young had attracted her in any way. He was about Brent's age and very presentable, but as far as her feelings were concerned, he left her cold. She couldn't imagine how Brent had read so much into the few times Jeff had laid his hand on her bare arm, but surely his crime hadn't been great enough to warrant the glacial glance Brent had given him as he had left? Jeff had gone quite pale and Sari's anger with her husband, never far below the surface, had simply boiled over when he had tackled her.

Some of her anger, but now directed against herself, seemed to remain in her fingers as she wrenched at the stubborn catch of her mother's necklace. It had never been easy to take off, and she wished belatedly she hadn't worn it. It wasn't as if she was particularly fond of it. She hated to admit she wore it chiefly to remind Brent of the night he had wrenched it from her neck. The necklace was all part of her confused plan to make him suffer, and she was sure he did, as his eyes frequently became fixed to it. Yet, somehow, she wished she had left it in her drawer this evening, as she couldn't forget the misery in his glance as he had noted it when she had joined him earlier to welcome their guests.

No matter how hard she tried the catch wouldn't give, but she decided against seeking Brent's help. In the mood he was in he might strangle her with it! With a final twist it did come off, but she realised it had broken again.

The next afternoon she made her way to the jeweller's

where Brent had taken the necklace the first time it had
been broken. He had mentioned the firm's name and
she hadn't forgotten. The necklace wasn't valuable and
the jeweller would undoubtedly remember, but if she
took it to the same place it might save someone else the
embarrassment of feeling he should explain to her that
the stones weren't genuine.

The assistant who attended her was very obliging,
especially when she mentioned who she was and
explained that the necklace had been here before.

'Couldn't you put on a new clasp this time?' Sari
asked.

The young man disappeared, to return in a few
minutes with another man who was obviously the
manager.

'Ah, Mrs Holding!' he bowed pleasantly. 'I know
your husband and explained to him that a new clasp on
such an old and valuable piece of jewellery might
remove some of its value. The present catch is very
delicate, as no doubt you are aware, and I'll admit,
after mending it the first time, I wasn't quite satisfied
with the results, but I advised him to seek your advice
before I did anything else.'

Sari looked at him with a faint frown. 'How—how
valuable would you say it was?'

He didn't hesitate. 'I couldn't guarantee how much
you would get if you tried to sell it, but to buy such an
article, even though it needs resetting, you might easily
pay in the region of ten thousand pounds.'

Why had Brent told her the stones were fakes? Sari
wondered all the way home, and failed to come up with
an answer. It wasn't as if he had ever attempted to steal
it, which would have been ridiculous, anyway,
considering all he had himself. He had given the
necklace back to her, it was the same one, the jeweller
had recognised it, and she couldn't understand!

She had intended asking him about it as soon as she
got in, but something happened to prevent her doing

this immediately. It was after six and there was a
message waiting for her. Brent wouldn't be in for dinner
and she wasn't to wait up for him.

This was the third time he had dined out in the last
two weeks and she supposed, as usual, he was
entertaining business clients. Since their honeymoon he
had frequently spent the evening in his study working,
and last night, hadn't Jeff Young said, albeit jokingly,
that Brent would wear them all out if he continued at
his present pace?

She had just thanked Carter and was turning away
when the telephone rang. Thinking it might be Brent,
she hurried to answer it, but to her utter surprise it was
her cousin Cilla. She hadn't heard from Cilla since she
had gone to live at Carnford.

'I hope you don't look as surprised as you sound,
darling?' Cilla purred.

Feeling it was senseless to pretend, Sari replied a little
flatly, 'I'll admit you were the last person I was thinking
of, but it's nice to hear from you,' she forced herself to
add politely.

'I just wondered how you are, darling,' Cilla laughed
lightly. 'Of course, I do see Brent from time to time, but
he doesn't seem to want to talk about you.'

'You . . .' Sari put her hand over the receiver while
she drew a deep breath in order to prevent herself
stammering. She often did this when she was disturbed.
It had began when her parents had been killed and she
had never been able to conquer the habit completely.
Beginning again, she tried to speak coolly. 'You see,
Brent?'

'Yes,' Cilla replied breezily, 'I'm actually seeing him
this evening. I helped him find you, remember? I think
that's why he likes to take me out occasionally.'

What on earth did Cilla mean? Why should Brent
believe he was obliged to take Cilla out? Sari gazed at
the telephone with glazed eyes, knowing the answer was
staring her in the face. Cilla was a model. She was also

an actress, with a fairly good idea how to get what she wanted. She was beautiful too, in a sexy, extravagant way. It didn't take genius to work out why Brent sought her company!

'You're a very lucky girl!' Cilla gushed, taking advantage of Sari's unhappy silence. 'Brent's so wealthy. That's why I knew you wouldn't mind my accepting the diamond bracelet he gave me.'

When Cilla rang off Sari felt ill. Cilla was triumphant, and perhaps she had every reason to be, with Brent taking her out and giving her expensive presents! Stumbling to her room, Sari flung herself on the bed, burying her stunned face in her hands. Brent had never given her anything. He had given her clothes and a generous allowance, of course. but he couldn't have known how often she had longed for a gift that wasn't strictly necessary.

He must have been too busy taking other women out and buying them things! And yet—Sari's hands clenched painfully as she pounded them distractedly against her pillows—hadn't she deliberately driven him into the arms of women like Cilla? Wasn't that simply the backlash of her own cruelty, her continual rejection of his every attempt to put things right between them? Hadn't she held him responsible for everything in order to absolve herself of all blame? She had tried to appease her own guilty conscience by making herself believe he had practically raped her and she had been helpless to prevent it.

But it hadn't been like that. Nor had it been the shameful affair she had tried to make it out to be. Like scales falling from her burning eyes, Sari realised that though Brent was definitely the more experienced, he might have been as incapable of avoiding what had happened as she had been. He might not love her now, but she suspected he had been halfway to loving her then, and perhaps, for the first time in his life, unable to fight the strength of his own feelings.

Neither could she have helped by clinging to him as she had done? Sari almost moaned aloud. Why had she always imagined that men found it easy to slam on the brakes? They were only human after all, the same as women.

Sari had told Carter she didn't want any dinner, but she realised he might grow anxious if she stayed in her room. Eventually she had a bath and dressed, then went to the lounge where she sat staring blindly at the television. She almost jumped out of her skin when Carter soberly announced a visitor and Santo walked in.

'Santo!' she breathed, dismay in her voice, because she still remembered how angry he had been with her.

'It's all right, Sari.' As Carter left them, he crossed quickly to her side, dropping a light kiss on her cheek. 'Please don't panic. I haven't come to embarrass you or try to entice you away from your husband.'

Her wide green eyes flickered doubtfully as, without waiting for an invitation, he sat himself down. 'If you did try and entice me, as you put it, I don't believe it would be because you loved me!'

He grinned wryly. 'You're getting nearly as sharp as Brent, although these days I forgive him, as he seems to be suffering enough—for some reason or another.'

Sari flushed. 'What did you want, Santo?'

'Look,' Santo hesitated, 'I gleaned from Carter that Brent isn't at home, but I've no wish for him to return and find me in his lounge. Will you come out for a drink or some coffee? I have a few things I'd like to say, but I promise to have you back within the hour.'

About to refuse, Sari suddenly shrugged. Why shouldn't she? What was there to stop her? In view of what she had learnt earlier she doubted if Brent would mind, and he needn't know. It was unlikely he would be back himself until after midnight. Knowing Santo as she did, she thought it unlikely that what he seemed dying to get off his chest would be very important, but what had she to lose by listening to him? And could anything be worse than sitting here, wondering what Cilla and Brent were doing?

She settled for coffee, and the small cosy café they found wasn't so very far away. Then Santo told her he was going to Italy for Christmas.

'There's a girl there,' he confessed, 'a family my mother wanted me to marry in to. I don't know, though,' he shrugged, 'since Brent made me understand the disadvantages of getting married at my age, I've put the idea of any permanent relationship from my mind, but there's no harm in looking, would you say?'

Solemnly Sari shook her head. 'Just as long as you refrain from doing more until you're sure the girl reciprocates your feelings.'

Santo had the grace to look slightly ashamed. 'I'm sorry I acted with you the way I did,' he burst out impulsively. 'I guess I got carried away by the thought of having a proper home of my own and imagined all I had to do to get it was to sweep you off your feet. That Brent succeeded where I failed, I'll admit took a bit of swallowing, but now that I've had time to get used to the idea of your being married to him—well, I find I don't mind nearly so much, and I hope you'll be very happy, Sari.'

He sounded so candidly sincere that Sari found herself smiling gently and squeezing his hand. 'When you return from your grandmother's, after Christmas, Santo, I hope everything will be fine between Brent and you. I know, after you finish at university, he's hoping you'll decide to join him in the business.'

'Thanks, Sari.' He jumped up quickly as she rose with a surprised glance at her watch. 'I know it's later than I meant it to be, but you don't know how good it's been, just talking to you.'

Santo said goodbye briefly on the doorstep and she was glad he didn't ask to come in. It wasn't really late, just after eleven, but all she wanted to do was to go to bed and hide her head, so there would be no danger of anyone guessing how unhappy she was.

Quietly she let herself in the house. She had told Carter not to wait for her, and although he had looked doubtful he must have taken her advice, because there was no sign of him. She was unprepared for the lounge door suddenly to be flung open and to find Brent standing there. A furious Brent, from the looks of him, with his hair rumpled as if it had been frequently subjected to agitated fingers and the glitter of anger in his eyes.

'What the hell have you been up to, at this time of night?' he attacked her. 'Where on earth have you been? Why aren't you in bed?'

'Do you know I wasn't?' Sari managed an indifferent shrug which she could tell incensed him.

'Don't ask stupid questions,' he snarled. 'You know I'm not allowed in that holy of holies you call your bedroom!'

'If you knock I always answer,' she asserted coolly, hoping he didn't notice how much she was trembling.

He ignored what she said with contempt, speaking between his teeth. 'I suppose you've been out with Jeff Young?' and, without waiting for an answer, 'He seemed pretty smug when I spoke to him today. God, I wish now I'd rammed that smile down his throat! He won't be looking as if he'd won the pools tomorrow, I can tell you!'

Sari stepped back, her heart pounding. Jeff Young had rung that morning, thanking her for a delightful evening. He had hoped she would allow him the pleasure of returning her hospitality soon. Still angry with Brent, she had thanked him more warmly then she might otherwise have done, but had naturally concluded that Brent would be included in any invitation which might arrive. Maybe she had sounded more enthusiastic than she had intended.

However, what right had Brent to criticise? Attempting to conceal her guilt with anger, Sari rounded on him. 'I haven't been anywhere with Jeff Young. If you must know, Santo called and we went out for a coffee . . .'

'Santo!' Brent's control blew up in fury. In two strides he reached Sari, grabbing her by the shoulders and dragging her to the lounge. When she stumbled and lost her feet, he didn't pause but swept her over the carpet, as though she was weightless. In the lounge, as he whipped her to her feet, he lifted his hand and slapped her face. Then, as she shrank from him with a petrified cry, he flung her on the settee and himself after her. With hands of steel he yanked off her jacket, then ripped her shirt from top to bottom, so that every button flew.

'You little bitch!' he raged, sparks leaping from his eyes. 'How dare you defy me like this?'

'Brent, please!' she began, but he stopped her voice with his mouth, punishing her in a way he never had before. He ground her lips against her teeth as her head was pressed back against the cushions, and she tasted blood. Yet, despite his brutality, the overwhelming feeling was still there, sweeping through them like fire, so instant and devastating that she felt his immediate response.

He must have realised what was happening as he suddenly sprang from her with a smothered oath. Taking a dazed advantage, Sari whispered through swollen lips, 'You're a fine one to talk— having just been out with another woman!'

'Another woman?' If she had stabbed him in the back he couldn't have straightened more swiftly. Whipping around, his face was suddenly despairing, whereas before it had been livid with anger. He made no attempt to deny her accusation. Instead he asked hoarsely, 'Who told you?'

'Cilla rang.' Sari wished desperately that she hadn't

mentioned Cilla, but the words kept tumbling out, 'She said you were taking her out to dinner and that you had bought her a diamond bracelet . . .'

For a long moment Brent was silent although a flicker of shock seemed to touch his face. Then he said slowly and flatly, 'What if I did?'

'It's your own business, I agree,' Sari's voice held little emotion either, 'But you had no right to criticise me. I've never done anything like that. Santo only wanted to talk to me. We were out just over an hour and I can assure you he's quite normal again. He realises he isn't in love with me and probably never was.'

'I'm sorry,' Brent muttered thickly, a white ring around his mouth but otherwise composed, 'but as you hate me, I don't suppose you mind who I take out, and Cilla is handy.'

'Yes,' she agreed hollowly, finding herself beginning to shake.

He didn't repeat his apology, but announced, with a harshness which jerked her dull glance back to him, that there was no point in talking any more and he was going to bed. As he said goodnight Sari was startled to see how haunted he looked and how his eyes seemed sunken in the greyness of his face.

Later she showered listlessly, on her way to her own bed, only half aware of what she was doing. She was finding it impossible to forget Brent's face, his tortured expression. Why had she such a feeling that he hadn't told her the whole truth? He had had so little to say about Cilla. Most men, if confronted by their wives regarding a girl they were having an affair with, would surely try to defend themselves? And why, if he was in love with someone else, had he attacked her so fiercely in the lounge? Remembering the savage passion of his kisses, she was suddenly sure they hadn't been the kisses of a man emotionally involved with another woman.

It was then that Sari knew she must do something.

She couldn't live with such uncertainty—and neither could Brent, if appearances were anything to go by. Stepping quickly from the shower, she paused only long enough to fling a thin négligé around her still wet body. Brent might hate her, it might be too late to wipe out the effects of her irrational behaviour, but if she did finish up wholly defeated, in a bleak future she might find some crumb of comfort in knowing she had tried.

Brent's rooms were alongside hers. What the staff thought of them sleeping apart she had long since given up wondering. Without knocking she apprehensively turned Brent's doorknob, opening the door a mere fraction. He was sitting on his bed, his head bowed in his hands. If she hadn't seen for herself, Sari would never have believed the great Brent Holding could look such a picture of dejection. But if she was startled by such a stance there was more to come. As he reared his head to stare at her, as she came slowly into the room, she was even more stunned by what she was certain was the gleam of moisture in his eyes.

Grimly he exclaimed, as shock caused her to pause abruptly, 'Well, have you come to gloat?'

Sari tried to speak, but suddenly, as he brushed an impatient hand over his eyes, tears were running down her own cheeks and with a choked cry she ran to him. Flinging herself on to her knees, she wrapped her arms around him, clinging to him desperately.

'Oh, Brent,' she sobbed, 'I'm sorry. Please forgive me for all the terrible things I've said. I love you so much, at times I've scarcely known what I was saying, but if you want Cilla, I won't stand in your way.'

'Want Cilla?' He froze, then convulsively lifted Sari on the bed, holding her so tightly she began finding it difficult to breathe. 'I never wanted Cilla or anyone else since I first set eyes on you,' he said hoarsely. His glance scorched her as he raised her face to gaze straight into her tear-drenched eyes. 'Never mind about

Cilla. Would you care to repeat what you just said about loving me?'

'I realised I loved you not long after you came to Carnford,' she confessed unevenly, 'and I've never stopped.'

'Oh, my darling,' he groaned, 'if only I'd had the sense to believe you!'

'I thought you only wanted to marry me because of what happened,' she faltered, 'because you feared there might be a baby.'

'That was merely an excuse,' he muttered bleakly. 'I wouldn't have minded if there had been one, believe me, but you were more important by far. I simply used the possibility of your being pregnant as a means of persuading you to marry me. I was convinced that you hated me, you see, and that I'd have to use some form of blackmail before you'd consent to be my wife. A divorce in a year's time was something else I dangled, but I hoped you would learn to love me long before then.'

Sari's eyes widened as she stared up at his gaunt face. 'You mean you never really wanted a divorce?'

His voice was harsh with remembered pain. 'I thought you were beginning to hate me instead of loving me, but I would never have let you go.' Tenderly he pressed swift, repentant kisses on her mouth and cheeks, apologising hoarsely for slapping her so brutally. 'I've been nearly out of my mind,' he said thickly, when Sari assured him she had been as much at fault and that she forgave him, 'You don't know the lengths I went to, to get you and keep you. I even made you believe your necklace was worthless, so you wouldn't think of selling it and using the money to escape me.'

'I found out about that,' she confessed hesitantly.

'You did?'

'Yes. I broke it again,' she admitted, 'and took it to the same man. He told me—but it doesn't matter,' she added hastily as Brent's eyes darkened despairingly.

'The catch is weak. I think eventually I might sell it and give Frank half to help with Carnford. I know Mother would rather I did something like that than leave it lying around doing nothing.'

'Can you ever forgive me?' he groaned.

'Easily,' she whispered huskily, her mouth moving sensuously against the hard brown skin of his neck. 'But you haven't explained about Cilla. I'm trying hard not to be jealous . . .'

'That's the last thing you need to be of her,' Brent's teeth snapped together. 'You remember I mentioned she'd helped me to find you, when you ran away from Carnford, and that she'd proved expensive?' As Sari nodded reflectively, he went on cynically, 'I realised instinctively that she knew where you might be, but merely taking her out didn't seem enough to jerk her memory. It wasn't until she began hinting about diamond bracelets that I began to understand what she was after. She had no difficulty at all with her memory, once one was on her wrist.'

Sari felt ashamed of Cilla yet puzzled. Brent obviously despised her distant cousin. Because she was sure of that, she found herself asking, 'So why did you take her out tonight?'

'She rang me at the office after lunch and asked me to meet her at the Savoy. It was about you, she said, but she refused to disclose anything more over the phone. When we met she insisted she couldn't talk on an empty stomach. I was so desperate about you I was ready to agree to anything, but all she told me afterwards was that she was worried about you as she believed you weren't happy. She swore you'd been in touch with her.'

Sari raised startled eyes. 'It was the other way round,' she told him dryly. 'Cilla rang me, this evening, just after I'd got in, to say you were taking her out—and to tell me about the bracelet.'

For a moment Brent looked like murder. 'I'm glad I

gave her short shrift. I don't flatter myself she wanted to start an affair, but whatever she was after, I left her in no doubt that she wasn't getting anything more from me.'

'I wish you'd told me about the bracelet yourself, though,' Sari said wistfully.

Bitterly he replied. 'My pride wouldn't let me, and it seemed all I had left. I believed if you knew how much I'd spent, you'd easily guess how crazy I was over you.'

'Oh, darling,' she moaned, her voice breaking, 'if only I'd guessed! You don't know how much I love you.'

'It's been agony,' he said hoarsely. 'On our honeymoon it was sheer bloody hell. Have you any idea how much I suffered? I've been going slowly insane,' he gazed at her with barely controlled passion in his eyes. 'I hope you realise you won't be going farther than this bed for a very long time.'

Sari's heart beat faster as she clung to him. 'Kiss me,' she begged.

But his lips, when he bent, merely brushed her bruised cheek again. 'I've been so crazy with jealousy over every man who so much as glanced at you,' he muttered harshly, 'but that's no excuse for hitting you. I've never hit a woman in my life.'

'Shush!' she breathed gently, her arms reaching round his neck, knowing she must make him forget. A small, wise voice whispered in Sari's ear that such a moment should be an occasion for joy, not regret. She moved a trembling hand to caress his lean cheek as she murmured softly, 'You have as much to forgive me for, but can't we forget and begin again?' As he hesitated, his eyes flaring darkly, she looked at him through teasing lashes. 'When are you going to stop talking and make love to me? I don't think I can wait much longer.'

She didn't have to ask twice. Almost before she had finished speaking, he was laying her back on the bed, removing their clothes, while his mouth claimed hers hotly. As he pushed the pillow out from below her head, passion leapt between them like a wild thing in which gentleness played no part. Both were blind and deaf to everything but the searing flame that engulfed them, bringing together their bodies with a feverish intensity.

Sari twisted uncontrollably, the prickling hair on Brent's chest driving her almost mad as did the driving hardness of his thighs. His hand slid underneath her hips, and as she melted into him, his grip tightened in his frenzy. She could feel her breath coming with his in brief shuddering gasps and felt her entire body clinging in wild response to him. The urgency within her mounted until she was overwhelmed by a sweet, stabbing agony that suddenly erupted in waves of ecstasy so intense that she cried his name as she was caught up in an unearthly force of exquisite, shuddering pleasure.

Later she became aware of Brent kissing her tenderly and murmuring gentle apologies for being so brutal against her soft lips. 'It's been so long, darling,' he brushed the damp hair off her hot forehead, his eyes and hands frankly adoring, 'and I've wanted you so much.'

She didn't try and hide that she felt exactly the same. 'I didn't think anything could be so wonderful,' she said shyly, 'I've only ever belonged to you, but I think this was better than the first time?'

His mouth quirked ruefully at the faint flush that coloured her cheeks. 'I hurt you then, didn't I? But,' he added wickedly, 'I promise it will get even better as from now on you're going to get plenty of practice, Mrs Holding.'

She smiled at him drowsily and happily, having no wish to argue. 'How about you?' she whispered, with a regrettably feminine curiosity.

Brent gazed at her lovingly as he continued caressing her, his hands gentle but threatening to send her into another spiral of delight. 'It's never been like this for me with anyone else,' he confessed, his slight smile fading as his voice thickened again, 'I've never been able to look at another woman since I met you, and nothing I've had before could compare with the feelings I experience when I'm with you. I suppose it's because I've never been in love before.'

'I thought,' Sari teased gently, 'you didn't believe in love?'

'I do now,' he growled, and as if to punish her for daring to taunt him, he allowed his mouth to trespass on areas his hands had been enjoying.

Sari immediately felt her bones turn to liquid as his hands and mouth went over her and he marvelled at the silky, inviting texture of her skin. There was no ending to their acute awareness of each other, and she felt herself begin to tremble as he spoke with a mounting urgency. 'Never stop loving me, Sari. I may be bad-tempered and arrogant and like my own way, but your love is the one thing I can't do without. If you are willing to be patient, I swear I'll try and reform.'

Softly Sari let her eyes and hands trace his well-loved features, remembering how, in the beginning, she had thought him all the things he had just quoted. Now she realised there wasn't a single thing about him she would have changed, even if she could.

'Oh, darling,' she murmured huskily, 'I love you just as you are. Unless——' she hesitated, smiling at him a little provocatively through the thick screen of her lashes, 'unless, perhaps, you're still inclined to talk too much?'

Brent laughed as he gathered her closer against his lean, hard body. 'That's a fault that can easily be remedied,' he growled as his mouth met hers passionately. And then he began to demonstrate, to Sari's complete satisfaction, that he was very capable of expressing himself with the help of only a very few words indeed.

Harlequin Plus

A WORD ABOUT THE AUTHOR

Margaret Pargeter's earliest memories are of her childhood in Northumberland, in northern England. World War II was raging, but in spite of the gravity of the times, she recalls, people always tried to find something to smile about. That memory, and that philosophy, have stayed with her through the years.

Short-story writing was a habit that began in her early teens, and after her marriage she wrote serials for a newspaper. When her children were in school she did several years of market research, which she believes gave her a greater insight about people and their problems, insight that today helps her in creating interesting plots and developing believable characters.

Today, Margaret lives in a small house in the quiet Northumbrian valley where she grew up. On the subject of writing romances, she is convinced of one thing: "It is not easy. But not the least among my blessings is the pleasure I get from knowing that people enjoy reading my books."

DISCOVER...

SUPERROMANCE

From the publisher that understands how you feel about love.

For a truly SUPER read, don't miss...

SUPERROMANCE

EVERYTHING YOU'VE ALWAYS WANTED A LOVE STORY TO BE!

Contemporary!
A modern romance for the modern woman — set in the world of today.

Sensual!
A warmly passionate love story that reveals the beautiful feelings between a man and a woman in love.

Dramatic!
An exciting and dramatic plot that will keep you enthralled till the last page is turned.

Exotic!
The thrill of armchair travel — anywhere from the majestic plains of Spain to the towering peaks of the Andes.

Satisfying!
Almost 400 pages of romance reading — a long satisfying journey you'll wish would never end.

SUPERROMANCE